B⚙⚙T

THE CREAKY
CREATURES

The BOOT series

BO⚙T

THE CREAKY CREATURES

SHANE HEGARTY

ILLUSTRATED BY BEN MANTLE

HODDER CHILDREN'S BOOKS

First published in Great Britain in 2020 by Hodder and Stoughton

1 3 5 7 9 10 8 6 4 2

Text copyright © Shane Hegarty, 2020
Illustrations copyright © Ben Mantle, 2020

The moral rights of the author and illustrator have been asserted.

A CIP catalogue record for this book
is available from the British Library.

ISBN 978 1 444 95879 9

Printed and bound in Great Britain by
Clays Ltd, Elcograf S.p.A

The paper and board used in this book
are made from wood from responsible sources.

Hodder Children's Books
An imprint of
Hachette Children's Group
Part of Hodder and Stoughton
Carmelite House
50 Victoria Embankment
London EC4Y 0DZ

An Hachette UK Company
www.hachette.co.uk

www.hachettechildrens.co.uk

For Oisín.

IS THAT Y●U, MR PIGGLES?

Ever since I woke with only two-and-a-half memories and my feet dangling in a grinder, I've had a few surprises.

263 surprises to be exact.

Here are some of them:

Surprise number 34: The first time I noticed human eyebrows. It's like you've glued furry caterpillars over your eyes.

Surprise number 56: The first time I saw a child sneeze and their head *didn't* shoot off like a rocket.

Surprise 109: *Everything* about human feet.

Most of all, I am surprised that there are always things left to surprise me.

Every time I think I've had *all* the surprises, something comes along that I didn't expect.

Sometimes it makes everything in me freeze or my screen just becomes two giant eyes trying to take it all in.

So, here is number 264 on my list of Things That Have Surprised Me Since I Woke With Only Two-and-a-Half Memories and My Feet Dangling in a Grinder: Mr Piggles trotting right past a side door of Dr Twitchy's Emporium of Amusements.

Mr Piggles was a robot pig I had met when I was looking for my friend Beth. Its owner brought me to their home to join her robot pets, but I climbed out of a window and escaped because her son wanted to turn me into a leprechaun.

I did *not* want to be a leprechaun.

I didn't want to be any kind of pretend creature with a silly hat and little red beard.

I just wanted to be Boot. I wanted to be *me*.

So I ran away.

I left behind that horrible boy.

I left behind the pretend pets.

I left behind Mr Piggles.

And I hoped never to see them ever again.

But here was Mr Piggles, metal trotters splashing through the puddles left by morning rain.

While talking to my newest, biggest and rustiest friend Rusty, I had spotted the robot pig passing the open door at the edge of Dr Twitchy's bowling alley.

"Is that you, Mr Piggles?" I asked in a low voice, half-talking to myself.

"Is that *who* Mr Piggles?" asked Rusty, whose long, broken arm rested on the top of a rack of dusty bowling shoes.

"That little pink pig robot outside," I said. "I know it. I met it before."

I was very surprised, but there was another feeling inside me. I felt a strange fizzing through my tummy wires. My head felt like it was as sloshy as a bowl of water.

I tried to push away the strange sensation and walked to the door for a look outside.

Rusty leaned over me to get a glance too. "A pig? Never saw a pig before." Rusty had spent a long time trapped in a Testing Lab, not allowed out. "I thought pigs had wings."

Mr Piggles didn't have wings, but it was different to how I remembered. There was a dent in its snout, just like when we met the first time, but it was worse than before – so bad that its nostrils were sideways, one on top of the other. And Mr Piggles was dirtier and had more dents and scratches than ever before.

Mr Piggles was quite broken. Just like I was broken, thanks to my cracked screen and the hole in my hip where a drawer used to be.

I heard Poochy bark behind me.

"RUFFF. RUFFFZZZZPPPPTTT."

My robot dog friend bounced out of control into the bowling alley. It did forward flips one after another, with its hair flying around and one eye flashing different colours.

Noke stormed in after Poochy. "Have you seen the mechanical mutt's control switch? It must have got knocked off when Poochy accidentally got hit by the pins in the bowling alley."

"When you used Poochy as a bowling ball? When you threw Poochy into the pins?" asked Rusty seriously, mouth of lightbulbs pulsing with each word.

"This is *not* the time to worry about silly little details," said Noke, on hands and knees, searching the long bowling lanes.

"Boot saw a pig," said Rusty. "A pig without wings."

From the door I watched Mr Piggles zigzag along the alley's walls, stopping every now

and again to push its dented snout into the damp gutters or small piles of rubbish.

"It's Mr Piggles," I said over my shoulder to Noke. "A robot pig I met before I met you. It's all alone."

"Are you sure it's the same pretend pig?" asked Noke, looking for Poochy's switch under a pile of knocked-over bowling pins. "All those things look the same. Like, when I first ended up on the streets it took me a while to realise all traffic lights were not the same ones, but different ones that just look the same. Although *all* traffic lights are very rude."

Poochy did another somersault. And yet another.

"No, it's definitely Mr Piggles," I said, my child-like voice rising because I did not like Noke telling me I might be wrong. "It had a dent in its snout, but it's worse now.

And it didn't have so many bumps and scrapes. And it was cleaner. But it's the same pretend pig."

Poochy somersaulted behind me, bouncing off the wall and floor.

My head still felt a bit swimmy and my tummy a bit fizzy. Maybe I had to recharge my solar batteries. I had been indoors all morning, hiding from the early rain. My batteries only had 30 per cent power left.

"There it is!" said Noke, sliding into a triangle of pins with a clatter.

Believing Noke had got a strike, the bowling lane trumpeted a triumphant tune. From among the scattered pins, Noke held Poochy's switch high, before ducking under the machine that swung down to sweep the pins away.

"Rusty, would you mind helping me?" asked Noke.

Poochy somersaulted once, twice and then – on the third somersault – Rusty whipped the loose, broken arm towards Poochy, catching the dog.

While Noke fixed the control switch to a bare patch on Poochy's belly, I watched Mr Piggles and tried to calculate what I should do.

Mr Piggles *oink*ed an electronic *oink* and trotted down the alleyway. There was no sign of any owner. It did not look like following Mr Piggles would lead to me having a green hat stuck to my head and a little red beard glued to my face.

I still had that strange sensation that made my head feel funny. But not funny in a way that made me want to burp a giggle.

Yet, for some reason I *needed* to know if the bent-nosed pig was lost – or had been thrown away.

I followed Mr Piggles.

F●LL●W THAT PIG!

Mr Piggles weaved through the maze of the city's alleys, sometimes stopping to *oink* an electronic *oink*, or to push its broken snout into a pile of rubbish before moving on again.

Was it lost? Had it been thrown out like so many of us?

Mr Piggles's wandering journey took me quite a distance from Dr Twitchy's. Eventually, I didn't recognise this part of the city, where the buildings crowded in particularly tightly and daylight hardly reached the ground.

The further I went from Dr Twitchy's, the more my wires began to tighten with worry.

I touched the jewel on my chest, glued there by Beth like it was a medal. Maybe it would give me strength. Maybe it would remind me of when

I was brave before. But I didn't want to get lost or claimed by a suspicious human who might bring me home – or feed me to a grinder.

"Where are you going?" a voice asked. I nearly fell over with shock, spinning around to see it was only Noke standing behind me, chunky eyebrows pressed together.

Poochy scrambled along behind, no longer

doing somersaults.

"You left Dr Twitchy's without even telling us,"
said Noke. "Did an earwig get into your head?
That happened to our friend Gerry once and he
thought he was a bowl of jelly for a whole week
until we realised what had gone wrong."

"I need to see what's happened to Mr Piggles,"
I said.

"You're following that pretend pork chop?" said Noke. "The damp must have leaked in through the crack in your face and made you crazy."

"RUFFFF," said Poochy, spinning around on the spot a couple of times.

"RUFFFZZZPPPTTTTTTTTTT."

Mr Piggles stopped briefly to examine an overturned cardboard box that had been dumped in the alley before trotting on again with a banana skin draped across its twisted snout.

"I need to follow that pig," I said, wobbling as I struggled halfway between a walk and a run. I always struggled when walking. Or running. Or anything in between.

"Yep, you must have a leaky face for sure," said Noke, catching up with me.

Poochy dodged around our legs but as Mr Piggles reached the top of the alleyway and looked around, Poochy got excited and chased up ahead.

Mr Piggles disappeared out of view.

I wobbled after, moving as fast as my egg-shaped legs would carry me. Which was not very fast.

Noke jolted along beside me, making grumpy electronic noises. "Boot, you could be grabbed by a human at any moment. Worse, *I* could be grabbed."

Leaving the alley, we were almost knocked over by a tall square robot carrying a large box. A round robot rolled past, nearly clipping my face as it headed the other way.

This street was frighteningly busy. Pressing against the wall for safety, we saw that people and robots crowded the pavement, vehicles passed in each direction and drones buzzed overhead.

Huge screens covered the sides of the skyscrapers above us, each of them flashing adverts for everything from sweet perfume to smelly cheeses, calming teas and explosive movies.

For a moment, it was almost too much for me to take in. I felt dizzy again. I needed to concentrate and search for Mr Piggles, who was lost among the metal and human legs moving this way and that.

"Where has Mr Piggles disappeared to?" I wondered.

"Never mind the bacon bot," said Noke. "Where's Poochy?"

The little dog had been here, bouncing around, only half a minute ago. Now, Poochy was nowhere to be seen.

"Where has that bionic barker gone?" asked Noke, pretending to be annoyed, but unable to hide the worry.

Through the noise of people and robots, drones and cars we heard an unmistakable sound.

"RUFF. RUFFFZZZZPPTTTT."

"Over there!" I pointed across the road, through the crowds and below the great flashing screens, to a boy. He was tall, but I guessed a little younger than Beth.

He had Poochy under his arm.

"**RUFF,**" said Poochy again, long tongue flapping loose. "**RUFFFZZZFFFLLPPTT.**"

The boy glanced around, as if checking to make sure no one was following. Holding Poochy tight, he slipped into a narrow, dark alleyway.

"He's pinched Poochy!" said Noke, dashing away to follow them.

Doing our best to look like normal, unfeeling robots – instead of the worried, panicky robots we were – we crossed the road while walking upright and stiff.

Reaching the

alleyway, with its high, graffiti-covered walls, we saw the boy stepping out the far end.

"RUFF," said Poochy, peering out from under the boy's armpit. "RUFFFZZZPPPTTT."

I stopped acting like a normal robot without feelings and ran quickly again, trying not to scratch my arms on the tight walls. Leaving the alleyway, I nearly crashed into Noke's back.

We had arrived on a quieter street – stretching out to meet streets at either end of a great square – and almost totally surrounded by tall, glass buildings. One of them had a three-storey high screen wrapped around it, an electronic billboard bursting with brightly coloured adverts.

But across from us – at the heart of the square – was a very strange sight.

Green. Lots of green. So much green I couldn't count it all. And I can count *lots* of greens.

A leafy park was squeezed in below the huge buildings that towered over every side of it. Glossy leaves, unruly bushes, lurching trees and bursts of colourful wildflowers spilled through the rusted railings holding everything in.

It was an explosion of nature in the middle of all the glass and concrete.

I have been surprised by a few things since waking in the grinder. This was surprise no. 265 and it felt as big as any of the others.

Yet, there was something else about this place. Something familiar …

"There's the Poochy pincher!" shouted Noke, spotting the boy walking towards a gate into the park, still holding our pet pal.

Before going into the park, the boy paused, turned and whistled. Mr Piggles appeared from under a big leaf flopping through the old railings, and followed obediently. "Got you!" said the boy, lifting Mr Piggles under the other arm.

He must be picking up loose robots, just as Noke had warned.

"Poochy will be nothing but furry bits and pieces if we don't save the little fella," said Noke.

This was all my fault. The fizz in my tummy felt more like a ball of electricity rising up inside me now. It took all my effort to push it back down.

"We have to find a way to rescue Poochy and get out without being mashed into metal dust," said Noke.

We crept forward, so tight to the railings that leaves slapped my face and soft branches brushed against my legs. We reached the open gate into the park, and beyond it I could see lush grass. On the gate was a faded iron sign:

IVY PARK.

Shafts of sunlight sliced through the skyscrapers and bathed the trees, casting dancing shadows across the grass. A path snaked from the gate towards the back of the gardens, turning out of view behind the overflowing trees and bushes and flowers of deep purples, reds and yellows. There was birdsong. There were insects. A blue butterfly wafted past my face and my eyes moved across the screen after it.

After so long in the city, these colours were such a shock. It felt almost as if the park – and all its life – didn't belong here in this city at all.

But again, there was something about it I thought I recognised. I just couldn't remember what.

"Let's creep in quietly," whispered Noke, as we stepped carefully through the gates. "We'll use the element of … BEAR!"

A huge brown bear rose up on hind legs before us, its lips curled to reveal fierce, robot-chomping teeth.

THUD. FLUMP.

Noke ran in one direction.

I wobbled in the other.

The bear followed me, its paws *thud-flump-thudding* on the grass as it got closer and closer.

Small birds scattered from the bushes I was running towards. I curled up and rolled in a ball across the grass, bobbling under a bush, twigs snapping. The hedge was too thick to roll any further.

I was stuck.

The bear slowed, stalking towards where I was hiding.

Thud.

Flump.

Thud.

Flump.

Its big bear face stared at me through the branches. I wanted to shut down completely. Maybe if I did that it would think I was too broken to eat.

Surely a bear wouldn't want to eat a robot anyway. But I guessed it would take a bite first, just to check.

The bear's lips pulled further back to reveal those thick fangs and it let rip with a blood-curdling…

"*Hee-haw.*"

Hee-haw?

Well, there was surprise no. 266.

"Hee-haw," the bear repeated, pushing its long snout through the bush and licking my face. A dry lick, like the tongue wasn't real. Then it sat on the grass, settling on its big bear behind.

It was only now I saw that two of its paws weren't actual paws, but fat, fluffy bedroom slippers shaped like bear paws but with soft floppy claws.

Ah, so *that* was why it walked with a *thud-flump*.

This was a lot of surprises all at once. There were more to come.

The bush next to me spoke.

"It's a robot bear," said the bush.

The bush sounded a lot like Noke, which confused me until I realised it *was* Noke, hiding beside me.

"The slippers are there to replace broken paws," said Noke.

The bear looked surprisingly realistic, even if I now saw that its eyes were a little too sparkly and its fur a bit too long and soft. And I didn't know a lot about bears, but I was pretty sure they didn't wear slippers.

"*Hee-haw,*" said the robot bear again. It turned and *thud-flumped* across the grass, its slippers squishing a patch of golden buttercups, before following the curving path out of view behind the overgrown greenery.

After checking to see if any other strange robots were nearby, we stepped out from the bushes.

"Why is a bear here?" I asked, peeling away a snail that had crawled on to the broken part of my hip. "Could it be a guard bear?"

"*Hee-haw,*" said the bear, out of sight.

"Or is it a guard donkey disguised as a bear?" I was so confused.

"Whatever is going on, it's weird," said Noke. "I mean, what else might be here? A shark in pyjamas? A sloth in comfortable pants?"

The bear had followed the path into the hidden

part of the park.

"I'm only going to follow it," said Noke, "because the boy took Poochy that way too. But if we turn a corner and get grabbed by a crocodile in boxer shorts, I'm going to be really annoyed."

Even though my tummy wires were fizzing again, I joined Noke on the curving, mossy path. It took us to a wide circle of grass, with an apple tree to one side. In the middle of the grass was a round pond, bubbles rising up in its murky water.

Everything was particularly overgrown here. The trees, shrubs and plants seemed to soak up the noise of the city – all the shouts and honks and drills and sirens – so they sounded like they were many miles away and not right on the other side of the rusty railings.

Something rustled in the trees near us. Something hiding in the dark, criss-crossed branches.

This so distracted Noke and me that we didn't

notice something creep up behind us.

I was grabbed by something far worse than a crocodile in boxer shorts.

A little girl.

MEL✷DY AND J✷RDAN

The girl gazed down at me with eyes so wide I was surprised they didn't fall out and plop on my head. Her mouth was wide open too. Her top two front teeth were missing, and I worried that the bottom two might fall out, along with her eyes.

I froze. Noke stopped too, one foot still lifted off the ground.

She was much younger than the boy we had seen. Her face was soft, her cheeks rounded with a splodge of pink in each one.

"I found a toy!" the girl cried out, her ponytail slapping against my face as she looked around. "And another old, scratchedy robot too."

The bear returned, lumbering over to sit beside her. *"Hee-haw,"* it said, just like a bear shouldn't.

I stayed frozen, my eyes nothing but blank

white circles and my face an unmoving line. I wanted to look like I wasn't turned on. Maybe the little girl would get bored and leave me alone.

"Turn on, toy," she demanded, speaking clumsily like young humans often did. "Turn on!"

The little girl shook me.

I did not like being shaken. I worried about my insides getting cracked or rattly.

Still, I didn't change. I didn't want to "turn on". I couldn't let this girl know I was not just any toy.

"Turn! On!" she yelled at me.

Without warning, Noke sprang to life and announced in a dramatic robot voice, "Stand back! I am an exploding robot and will explode in a big robot explosion!"

The girl screamed.

"Boom!" said Noke, not sounding at all like an explosion.

Screaming again, the girl dropped me on the soft grass and ran away.

The bear *hee-haw*ed and followed after her, slippers flapping, *thud-flump-thud*.

I lay on the grass, trying not to move even as Noke stood over me. "How's my Favourite Funtime Pal?"

There was no point in pretending any more. I blinked, stood awkwardly, wiped soil from my screen and checked myself over for dents.

Thankfully the only scratches on my body were the ones that had been there before.

"Are those the scary robots, Melody?" the boy asked, arriving on the path, still holding Poochy in his arms while Mr Piggles trotted around his legs. The girl – Melody – hid behind him.

"Yeah, Jordan," said Melody, sniffling into her sleeve. "Don't get too close. The rubbery one is explodey."

"*Rubbery!?*" exclaimed Noke, insulted. "I should explode just for you calling me that."

Melody hugged the chest of the bear for comfort.

"*Hee-haw,*" said the bear.

"Explodey ...?" said Jordan, with a curious smile. "Don't know about that. Robots are made not to explode. You know, around us anyway. So no need to cry about it, Melody."

"I'm *not* crying!" insisted Melody, definitely crying.

I felt trapped. Poochy was right there in front of us, but the boy – who, while not yet Beth's age, was tall and strong – had a confident grip on our doggy friend.

But something about his smile, and the way he protected the girl, told me he didn't want to turn me into a leprechaun. His face seemed warm, like Beth's. Like a good human. Like he was interested in us, but not in a way that meant he would tear us apart. Or glue silly red beards on our faces.

But I still had to be careful, so I said the one thing I had been made to say.

"I AM ROBOT-O-FUN, YOUR FAVOURITE FUNTIME PAL."

The boy smiled wider and took half a step closer.

"Are you two robots lost?"

"I AM ROBOT-O-FUN, YOUR—"

"We can drop the act, Boot," said Noke, waving a hand to tell me to stop. "And what's up with you, Poochy? We're here trying to rescue you but you're having a holiday in a human armpit."

"**RUFF,**" barked Poochy.

"**RUFFFFSSSPPPTT.**"

"You two are *crazy*," said Jordan. "What is going on with you?"

Again, he looked amazed and interested, rather than scary and mean. We were not like most robots – but I sensed Jordan and Melody might not be like most humans.

Mr Piggles snuffled through the grass, looking up with an earthworm wriggling on its rattling, bent snout.

"Maybe they're more thrown-away pets?" asked Melody. Her eyes had dried up a bit and she was smoothing down the damp patches of fur on the pretend bear.

"We're no one's pet. Not yours. Not *anybody's*," insisted Noke.

"Who owns you then?" asked Jordan.

"*No one*," replied Noke, insulted. "I'm *me*. And

so is Boot." Noke realised how silly that sounded. "You know what I mean."

"You followed this little guy in here, so I'm guessing the dog was with you," said Jordan, looking at Poochy, whose tongue was hanging loose and whose fringe was flopped over one eye while the other flashed crazily. "Good dog. You can go back to your friends now."

Jordan put Poochy down. The digital doggy did a headstand, fell over and then bounced back to us.

Noke petted Poochy's mangy fur. "Next time you run off like that, we'll leave you in whatever damp armpit you jump into."

Jordan laughed again. "This is nuts."

"Leave my nuts out of this," said Noke. "I gave them a fresh squirt of oil only last week."

"Listen, we're not going to do anything bad to you, if that's what you're worried about," said Jordan. "We're not going to scrap you or steal you. I've already got a robot a bit like you at home. Stupid thing was my dad's until he didn't want it any more. We didn't get a new one."

"Our dad says we don't have the money," said Melody, and Jordan gave her a glance that I guessed was a silent way of saying he didn't like her giving that information away.

"Anyway, it's *so* slow," he said. "And scratched. And annoying. I won't even bring it out, it's so useless. But we're still not going to steal you."

"Do you hear that, Boot? Now he's saying we're not even worth stealing,"said Noke. "I've not been so insulted since the day a child on the street thought I was a bin and tried to shove an ice-cream wrapper in my mouth."

"You see, I said this was *nuts*," repeated Jordan, face wide with surprise.

In the undergrowth behind the boy, something scurried within the branches of the trees and shrubs that crowded the edge of the grass. A shadow moved one way. Then the other. There was a rustle of movement.

Jordan noticed me look at it.

Noke leaned into me. "We have Poochy. Let's go home."

But I wasn't really listening to Noke. Beyond the pond, at the edge of the circle of grass, I saw a wooden bench, its seat warped a little and its paint flaking. Overgrown leaves had begun to snake around it, so much that it looked like it would eventually be lost completely in the green.

I recognised that bench.

I finally recognised this park.

I'd come here with Beth and her grandma.

The leaves shook again, as if something was

straining to escape.

"Definitely time to go," said Noke urgently.

"Is this your park?" I asked Jordan and Melody.

"Kinda," said Jordan. He pointed up towards one of the tallest buildings that loomed over the park, one with grids of grey concrete and dull glass from the bottom to the very top. "Melody's my sister. We live in an apartment at that window right there."

I couldn't tell which window it was. There were so many.

"So, this is sorta our garden," continued Jordan. "We used to have loads of gardens around here, but they all got torn up. There was a park over there where that twisty building is now. And another smaller garden over there, but they put a building there too, where the big screen is."

The big screen in the city outside the park was flashing an advert about coffee, with a sign with an orange circle and a white sideways triangle.

A sign that was once a clue for me to find Beth.
A woman with straight, ice-white hair that cut
across one eye sipped the coffee then winked at the
watching world.

"I liked that garden," said Melody, putting the

bear's ragged hair into a small, tight ponytail. "It
had a swing."

We had swings at Dr Twitchy's. I couldn't
imagine someone tearing them down to put a
tower there instead.

I shivered. Inside. From my belly right up to my head. Was I breaking after all that running, after being picked up, after being shaken by a little girl?

"This is it now," said Jordan, gesturing at the life all around. "The last place that's not glass or metal."

"There's nothing wrong with being made of metal," said Noke, insulted.

"Sorry," said Jordan, holding his hands up as an apology. "And again, *you two are crazy*."

There was another rustle in the bushes. Something alive in there.

"Don't show them the others, Jordan!" said Melody, concerned.

Others? I wondered.

Jordan shook his head, but not angrily. "Well, that's given away the secret, Melody." He looked at us. "Do you want to see 'em?"

Noke was right up beside me. "Noke's Rules of

43

the Street, number 81: always listen to Noke when Noke says it's time to run away."

I looked at that bench again and when I did I could suddenly picture the days I came here as bright and fresh as if it had only been yesterday. Before Grandma was sick. When she and Beth sat on that very bench and laughed and chatted and I waited patiently for them because I was just a toy robot then.

That was a happy memory and I didn't want to leave it behind just yet.

"Yes," I said. "We want to see them."

PET RESCUE

Jordan stuck two fingers in his mouth and whistled.

The leaves shook as if the bushes themselves were going to rip from their roots and pounce forward. Animals burst through the branches, scrambling over the grass.

Very *strange* animals.

A unicorn, half my size, with a multi-coloured horn chipped at the top. It didn't walk or trot, but bounced on four straight legs, its neat mane flopping while colours moved through it like rainbow waves. It had a button where its left eye should be.

A hamster so round and soft it looked like a walking fur explosion. Its eyes were huge and wide and when it looked at me, the pupils

swirled slowly like miniature galaxies. I was not programmed to want to pet any hamsters. I *really* wanted to pet that hamster.

And with a sound of cracking twigs and shaken leaves, a final robot creature emerged. It was lumpy and awkward, with a small head on a short neck and a long tail dragging behind.

A dinosaur of some sort, it was yellow and purple and hardly much taller than Noke – but much wider. Slowly, with a click and clack of turning gears – its neck grew, pushing its head up as it grew taller and taller and taller still until it loomed higher than anybody there.

It was a brontosaurus. A mini robot brontosaurus.

Without warning, its neck dropped and swung down towards me, forcing me to duck, as its head flopped and rose and dropped and dragged across the ground, bumping Noke before rising at last to loom unsteadily over me. Its long, thin and very weak neck clicked and clacked as its face wobbled before mine. I thought it would lose control and knock me over. Instead, it spoke.

"Hello," said the brontosaurus in an Irish accent. "My name is Sprout. I like plants."

I was sure real brontosauruses didn't say *"hello"*. I was sure they didn't say *anything*. And I was certain they weren't Irish.

"Watch out for Sprout," said Jordan. "That neck doesn't work too well." Jordan pulled a small rubber ball from his pocket and launched it to the edge of the park. Sprout scrambled after it, with the neck whipped back against its body.

"And I thought you humans were weird," said Noke. "Which you are. Very weird. You can't even unscrew your own toes."

"We found Sprout in a dumpster, with its head just hanging out of the top," said Jordan. "And Herman the hypno hamster was in a soggy shoe box."

Herman looked at me, its eyes swirling gently. It was hypnotically cute. I wanted to snuggle it. I had never wanted to snuggle *anything* before.

"Are you all right, Boot?" said Noke. "Your eyes have gone all twirly."

I stopped them twirling.

"Someone threw these pets out," said Melody, putting yellow ribbons in the bear's hair. "Someone even threw Slippers away. His back two paws were gone. Just wires and stuff hanging out everywhere. Poor Slippers."

"*Hee-haw*," said Slippers the bear.

"We stole our dad's slippers," said Jordan. "We'd bought them for his birthday so, you know, technically they were kinda ours to take anyway."

Sprout came back with the ball in its mouth, even though the brontosaurus's head was hanging down in the grass. Jordan threw the ball and Sprout chased after it again, nearly clobbering the unicorn as it bounded past.

"Killer was in a bag, just launched out of a car on to the side of the road," said Jordan.

"Killer?" asked Noke, raising an eyebrow.

"Killer the Unicorn."

"I called her that," said Melody proudly.

"When I get home I'm changing my name to Killer," said Noke. "No one will laugh at me then."

Noke stepped back and stumbled over Mr Piggles. The kids laughed. My face lit up in a bright sunny smile too. I didn't feel the fizz of broken wires now, but a surge of giddiness.

There was a gurgle in the water. A fat bubble rose to the top.

"Oh, and we can't forget about Sucky," said Jordan, darting over to the pond.

A slithering tentacle, covered in suckers, slapped down on the pond's concrete edge. Then another tentacle. And a third, but this one was the tube of a vacuum cleaner with the sticky bit of a toilet plunger fixed to it.

Two blinking eyes peeped out of the water, followed by the rest of an octopus climbing out on to the grass and up a tree. Then it vanished into the background. It could camouflage itself completely – all except for the toilet plunger tentacle, which didn't disappear, just looked like it was floating on its own.

The robot octopus popped back into view again, stretched between two branches, its tentacles tight. It let go of one branch, swung down and slid back into the pond with hardly a splash.

I had a question mark where my face should be.

"It's a robot, but it can do amazing camouflage like a real octopus," said Jordan. "We found it in a drainpipe."

"I think Sucky was flushed down a toilet," said Melody. "A *very* big toilet."

Jordan chuckled. "We fixed Sucky up as best we could, like all of the others. It's not perfect, but we do our best."

These kids were kind. They were not broken like many other humans.

Mr Piggles went *oink* as a spider crawled up one twisted nostril and dropped out of the other one.

"People want pets without the problems, you see," said Jordan. "That's what it actually says on the boxes they come in. *Pets Without The Problems.*"

"Pets without the poo is what they mean," said Melody.

Jordan laughed at that, but quickly became serious again. "Just cos they got broken or their owners got bored, they got dumped for a new pet. Or robot. Or whatever."

That sounded a little like what happened to me. And what happened to Noke. And what happened to so many robots.

I felt bad again, just like that, like bits of me wanted to stop working. My head wanted to shut down. My legs wanted to stop holding me up. Was I was breaking inside?

I needed something to make that feeeling go away. I thought of my happy memory here.

"I was here before," I announced.

"Before?" asked Jordan.

"With Beth," I said, walking to the bench and running the four chunky fingers of my hand over its flaking red paint. Some of the paint came away. I didn't like that so I stopped touching it.

"Beth was Boot's owner," Noke explained.

"It was different here then. There are so many more buildings now," I said. "That's why I didn't remember this place at first. But I remember this bench. Beth and her grandma came here three times."

I held up the stem of a flower poking through the gaps in the bench, and it drooped under the weight of its petals. It was purple with dark streaks of yellow exploding outwards. A bee bounced between flowers in the bushes and flew towards the one I held, hovering as it looked to see if it was interesting enough.

"When were you here?" asked Jordan.

"Before Beth's grandma got sick," I said.

"Before I changed."

My head felt swimmy again, like it was under the pond water with Sucky the octopus. Should I tell them how I was feeling? I didn't want them to think I was broken.

"Yeah, what happened to you?" said Jordan, stooping to stare into me, like he was trying to see my insides through my screen. "Does your old owner know you're like this? That you're really different? *Amazing*, and different. What happened to you two? What did you mean that girl Beth *was* your owner? Did she throw you away?"

For a moment I thought it must be too much for me. All this excitement. All these surprises. Because I began to shake. My belly shivered. My head quivered. My hands drummed against my hips.

But it wasn't me shaking.

It was the ground.

"What's that?" asked Melody, pointing at a

mound of dirt moving through the ground at speed.

Something was coming straight for us.

GROUND-BOT BOTHER

The thing burrowing through the soil was getting closer. The ground was getting shakier.

Mr Piggles's broken snout rattled.

Killer the unicorn bounced unsteadily and landed horn-first in the grass.

Sprout the brontosaurus's head swayed and dropped and vibrated on the grass. "I l-l-l-l-l-like p-p-p-plants."

Insects rose from the shuddering flowers as petals were shaken free.

The mound ran up to us until it bumped against Slippers's slippered claws and stopped dead. Ribbons shook loose from the bear's fur.

A thin periscope thrust up from the soil, through a clump of buttercups. A single electronic eye at the top of the periscope swivelled around quickly, as if in a great hurry. It looked at Slippers's big teeth and made a little meep in alarm before disappearing underground again.

"What *is that*?" asked Jordan, jumping over to where it had been.

The burrower moved towards the edge of the path, pushing up a small ridge as it did. Stopping, the eye appeared again and blinked while making a series of snapping noises like it was taking pictures.

"Ground-bot," Noke said.

"A what-bot?" asked Melody, her voice trembling.

The eye dropped back into the soil and began to tunnel a curve that followed the edge of the path, popping up again at the bench. It snapped some more pictures.

"What does it want with the bench?" I asked, feeling ever so shaken now.

Meep, went the ground-bot and disappeared again. It popped up at a tree to our right and we watched as the tree started to rock a little, then a lot. Leaves fell. It creaked and cracked.

"Hey, stop that," said Jordan, grabbing a large twig as if ready to strike.

Meep, went the ground-bot, once more retreating underground. The tree stopped swaying, and the ground-bot tunnelled away again, the trail it left on the surface getting flatter and flatter until it disappeared.

There was no more shaking. Mr Piggles's snout stopped rattling.

"I don't like it," said Melody, her face wobbling again, a bit like mine did but with more wrinkles and leakiness.

"Is it gone?" Melody asked, hugging the unicorn with one arm and cradling Herman the hypno-hamster with the other. Herman's eyes were swirling like a whirlpool after all the shaking.

"No need to worry," said Noke, checking to see if either eyebrow had fallen off. "A ground-bot won't harm humans."

My insides felt fiery. I touched my belly. Was I getting too hot?

"And a ground-bot doesn't care about robots

either," said Noke, waving a reassuring hand at me. "It only cares about the soil. And the roots. And the trees and plants and all those things in here."

"What, like a collector or something?" asked Jordan.

"Sort of," said Noke, checking that all fingers were where they should be. "A ground-bot collects information. On everything that's in a place. What might be in the way. What needs to go. Would you look at that, my little finger almost screwed right off in all that racket."

"What do you mean it checks 'what needs to go'?" asked Jordan, lowering the branch.

Noke screwed the finger in and gave it an extra turn to be sure it was on properly. "What needs to get dug up. Or pulled down. Whatever."

Melody's lower lip trembled.

Jordan dropped the branch, grabbed Noke firmly by the shoulders and forced the robot to

give him attention.
Noke's whole face
raised with creaky
surprise.

"What are
you saying?"
asked Jordan.

"The way you
talked about all the
buildings and the parks and
the way humans always need something new ... I
thought you already knew," said Noke.

"What is the explodey robot saying, Jordan?"
asked Melody.

"I'm saying," said Noke, "that someone's about
to tear this park down."

"No!" said Melody, through a choked sob.

Jordan let Noke go, walked slowly towards the
bench and slumped on it. The bench groaned a
little, as if it hadn't been sat on for a long time.

I felt that burning in my wires again, so much stronger than anything else. Stronger than any thoughts or ideas or calculations in my head.

"I thought you had figured all that out," said Noke, checking toes now. "That there was a park over there and over there and over there and now they're all gone. This one is next. I'm no maths bot – although I do a mean multiplication if you ever need one – but that just adds up."

"They can't," said Jordan, standing as if ready to confront someone – or something – about this.

Melody let out a little sad sob and used Herman the hypno-hamster to wipe a tear from her cheek.

As if sensing the mood, the robot pets were calm. Killer was standing still with the chipped horn dripping clods of soil. Sprout the brontosaurus laid its head on the grass. Slippers didn't *hee-haw*. Mr Piggles didn't *oink*.

Even Poochy had stopped running in circles

and was just lying down, head in its paws, tongue hanging loose on the grass.

It was so quiet I could hear the noise of the traffic and the city intrude. The huge screen glimmered bright light in the corner of my vision. The burning in my wires felt like it was spreading down through my legs.

Slippers was standing too close to me, its shadow over me, its fur almost tickling my shoulders.

"This is all we have left," said Jordan. "They can't destroy everything. They can't keep digging everything up till there's nothing left."

My head felt swimmy again, like the time I was washed down a rainy drain and couldn't stop myself.

I was getting so hot.

The world got blurry.

No, it wasn't the world that had gone blurry.

It was my vision.

It was not working properly. *I* was not working properly.

So I did the only thing I could.

I ran away.

RUN AWAY

I left them behind, moving straight across the grass, scattering butterflies, squishing a clump of buttercups and feeling very bad about it.

Still, I kept going until I reached the gates and walked straight into a pair of legs.

I looked up. A woman stood over me, in a long winter coat, an orange woollen hat tight on her head, carefully holding a coffee cup, fingers half covering that symbol of the orange circle with a piece of cake in it.

"Be careful, I'll spill my coffee," she said quickly, like she was in a hurry to speak. "A robot, huh. Where is this thing's owner?"

I couldn't let yet another human know that I wasn't owned by anyone. That I wasn't a normal toy robot.

I made my face almost blank again. Just
rectangular eyes and a smile that I had to force,
like it was made of steel.

"I AM ROBOT-O-FUN ..." I started to say as
mechanically as I could.

I couldn't finish the sentence. My words failed

me. My cartoon smile drooped.

"YOUR FAV—"

I had to go.

I wobbled around her legs, forcing Coffee Woman out of the way. A splash of coffee dropped on my shiny head, a thin drip running down my screen as I left the park.

I needed to get myself fixed.

THE MAGIC NUMBER

"What is going on with my Favourite Runaway Pal?" asked Noke, finding me back at Dr Twitchy's Emporium of Amusements, hiding between an Air Hockey game and Space Invaders.

Red, Rusty and Gerry were already standing over me, worried.

"Boot says you met a killer unicorn and an invisible octopus and two kids with a floppy dinosaur," said Red. "Is Boot's brain a bit scrambled?"

"Oh, all that stuff's true," said Noke. "I can't believe you didn't mention the bear in bedroom slippers, Boot."

"I think my tummy has a fire in it," I said. "And my head is swimmy."

"Oh, that's very bad," said Gerry. "It sounds like

what happened before my head started falling off."

Gerry's head had fallen off a couple of times recently. Noke had suggested replacing it with a bowling ball, but Gerry didn't like that idea and wanted to keep the same head, but just wanted it to stay between the shoulders rather than rolling across the floor.

Was *my* head going to fall off and roll across the floor?

"Do you need my heart?" asked Rusty, whose heart had broken once. We replaced it just before it was too late.

"You're very kind, but that would not be much help to Boot," said Red, placing a warm hand on Rusty's broad shoulder.

"But what if I stop working?" I shouted. Actually shouted. My cartoon face had very angry cartoon eyes on it. The others all took a step back, a bit shocked at my outburst.

Was this what anger feels like? Shouty and fiery?

"Your face has gone a bit red," said Noke, and when I held my silver-green hand up in front of me, it was bathed in a red glow from my screen.

"It sounds like you have been through a strange and busy morning," said Red in that gentle, chanting voice while calmly sitting on the floor opposite me. "Perhaps you have overloaded your systems."

I shook my head a little, and while I didn't

shout my voice was still very firm. "I've been through strange and busy days since coming here, but I didn't feel shouty and fiery like this before. And Noke was with me this morning but doesn't seem broken. Are you?"

"Apart from picking earthworms out from between my toes," said Noke, pulling a foot off to scrub it, "I'm perfect. But you know me. Indestructible."

One of Noke's toes fell off and clanged to the floor.

The anger left me as suddenly as it had arrived, like water draining out of a sink. All that was left was a feeling of heaviness, of helplessness. Of sadness.

"I don't want to break completely," I said.

"Are you sure we shouldn't try swapping heads?" asked Gerry.

I drew a big cartoon X on my face.

"How about asking Digits?" suggested Noke, sticking the toe, and then the foot, back on.

Digits? I wondered.

"Oh, yes, Digits has the magic number," said Gerry.

What was the magic number?

"We said we would only use it in emergencies," said Red, who I noticed had got a touch warmer, and a little redder at the mention of this idea. That was never a good sign.

"Boot's head is about to explode," said Noke. "I think that counts as an emergency."

My face showed a shower of sparks.

"OK, it won't explode," said Noke, trying to reassure me. "It'll maybe just smoke a little bit."

The fire in my tummy got even more fiery.

"What is Digits?" I asked. "What is the magic number?"

"Follow us," said Noke.

DIGITS

They took me through the many rooms of Dr Twitchy's, which was such a warren that despite all this time I had yet to visit each one. Which meant I had yet to meet every robot that lived here.

We passed an old pit full of soft balls that children used to dive into and disappear.

A pair of robot eyes on stalks

popped up and watched us go by.

"Hi, Boggles," said Noke.

A thin, metal hand pushed through from the colourful balls and gave a little wave at us. Rusty waved back, long broken arm dragging across the balls so that a couple bounced free. The robot dipped down under the balls again.

"Bye, Boggles," said Noke.

"Some of the clever robots who have found a home here just like to keep to themselves," said Red. "Some are too scared after being rejected. Some are upset at having no memories after getting the Wipes."

The Wipes was something that happened to robots when their memories were wiped clean before they were thrown out. This had happened to me. It was very scary.

"Some robots just want to be left alone with a little oil to keep them moving and a plug or a pile of batteries to keep them in energy," said Red.

"Digits was a maths bot, used to solve very difficult sums," said Noke. "But something went wrong."

"Now Digits doesn't say much, except one thing," said Gerry.

"The magic number," said Noke. "We only used it once and, well, let's just say it didn't go so great."

Noke and Red looked at Gerry.

"It wasn't my fault it was nearly a disaster," said Gerry.

Disaster?

I heard an electronic voice coming from a small dark store room in the farthest, grimiest corner of Dr Twitchy's. It was a woman's voice that had been recorded from a real human once upon a time. It was speaking numbers. One by one. As if they weren't connected to each other.

"5," it said, then paused. "0," and another pause.

"Digits has the magic number," whispered Red.

"I very much hope it will be the answer to your problem."

"And not be a disaster," said Gerry chirpily. "Not a disaster at all."

The store room was lit only by a thin, green glow, casting an eerie light on shelves that were bare except for a few small paintbrushes, a bottle of window polish, a stiff mophead and dusty cobwebs.

"5," said the voice, and as my vision adjusted to the low light I saw a robot, hardly as tall as my egg-shaped legs, made out of a pile of boxes – two small boxes for legs, one large one for the body, a wide one for a head.

The green glow was coming from its face, which was a screen with numbers flashing on it.

"9," it said and a nine appeared flashing on the screen.

"Hello, Digits," said Red.

Rusty gave Digits a wave too.

"9," said Digits, turning around and looking up at everyone.

"You're looking well," said Noke. "Must have a fresh set of batteries in there, am I right?"

"9," said Digits, and I think it was saying *yes*.

"You must be wondering why we're here," said Red.

"5," said Digits, the number popping up on its screen.

"Well, our friend Boot has a problem."

I gave a little wave to Digits.

"0," said Digits.

"Boot's broken," said Gerry. "Or breaking. Or about to break. Or one of those. Maybe all of them."

"5," said Digits sadly.

"We'd like to use the magic number, please," said Red.

"9!" said Digits.

"Yes, I know it was a disaster last time," said Noke.

"9!"

"It *will* be better this time," said Gerry.

"9?" said Digits.

"I will supervise everything," said Red, and this seemed to calm Digits a little.

I still didn't know what was going on. What did this little robot – stuck saying these numbers over and over – have that could possibly make my insides better? What magic number was there that would fix me?

The question marks where my eyes should be must have given away my confusion, because Noke explained things to me.

"When we first found Digits, we thought those numbers were just the babbling nonsense of a broken robot with the Wipes."

"5," said Digits, shaking its boxy head.

"But Gerry came to say hello one day and when Digits said the magic number it triggered something in Gerry."

"It triggered my phone," said Gerry, whose head could make phone calls. I sometimes used Gerry's phone to contact Beth.

"0," said Digits.

"The numbers made a call," said Red. "To a helpline. A robot helpline. It was a bit of a surprise."

"5," said Digits sternly.

"And yes, Digits, it was a disaster," said Noke. "But today will be different, I'm sure. Because we just want to help our pal here."

Digits looked at me, moving up close, little boxy head tilting upwards to look at me better. Its green glow bathed my screen, and I could see the crack in my face in the corner of my vision. Could Digits see that I was broken on the inside too?

Then Digits spoke not just one number. But a long number.

"505 999 505."

Gerry's head made a phone call.

MECA R⚙B⚙ C⚙RP⚙RATI⚙N HELPLINE

Someone answered.

"Hi, you've reached the Meca Robo Corporation Helpline," said a cheery man, his voice coming from Gerry's mouth. "We put a human touch on your robot problem. My name is Dean. How may I help you today?"

"I'll pretend to be human," said Noke, putting a blocky hand over Gerry's mouth so the man couldn't hear. "It's easy. All I have to do is imagine what it would be like to have a sponge for brains."

We each crowded in to hear better. Rusty's broken arm rested on my shoulder and it felt nice, like Rusty was comforting me.

"Hey there, Dean, what about that weather we're having?" said Noke, talking directly into

85

Gerry's mouth almost as if Dean the Helpline Man was a small person hidden inside. "Sometimes there is rain in some of the sky and no rain in other parts of the sky. Wild, right?"

Noke winked at us as if to say this was going *very* well.

"Umm, OK, right ..." said Dean. "So, what robot problem can I help you with today?"

"Yes indeed," said Noke. "I am a robot ..."

"Excuse me?" said Dean the Helpline Man.

"I mean, I *have* a robot," said Noke and then tried to laugh to pretend it was a jokey mistake. "Ha. Ha. Ha. Ha," laughed Noke, sounding exactly like a robot might if it was trying to laugh.

"Ha. Ha. Ha."

"Get yourself together, Noke," whispered Red.

My face was getting *very* wobbly again. I looked up at Rusty, and Rusty looked down at me, big lantern eyes brightening with concern.

Seeing this seemed to make Noke more determined and focused.

"I mean to say, Dean, my good human man, my robot is malfunctioning and I am hoping you can help me fix it."

"OK," said Dean brightly again. "What kind of model is it?"

"It's a Robot-O-Fun. Everybody's Favourite Funtime Pal," said Noke.

"Ah yes, we know it well," said Dean. "A very popular model."

That made me feel a bit better.

"Well, it *used* to be popular," continued Dean. "No one buys them any more."

That didn't make me feel better.

"And what's wrong with your Robot-O-Fun?" asked Dean.

Everyone looked at me. I wasn't sure how to answer that. Everything seemed wrong. Yet nothing I could point at. Except my face and tummy. So I pointed at my face and tummy.

"It's feeling very strange," said Noke.

"*Feeling* strange?" asked Dean the Helpline Man, because robots were not supposed to feel *anything*.

"Acting strange, I mean," said Noke. "Yes, definitely just acting. No feelings. Not like me. No, sir. I have plenty of normal human feelings inside my totally human body with all its soft human bits."

"Uh-huh," said Dean, confused.

"And dangly bits too," said Noke, warming to the idea of pretending to be human. "Can't forget all the dangly bits us humans have."

"5," said Digits, sounding like it already was a

disaster.

"Okaaayyy … so, what kind of strange things is your robot doing?" asked Dean.

How could I explain it without using words and being heard by Dean? I pointed to the ceiling.

"It's up," said Noke.

I pointed at the floor.

"And down," said Noke.

"Riiigght …" said Dean, who was sounding less and less chirpy. "Maybe you could reset your Robot-O-Fun. There's a button in its left ear hole. A small one, hard to see. If you have something thin, like a paper clip or a pin, you could use it to press that."

Red, Noke and Gerry peeked into my earhole and murmured to each other. I didn't even know I had a button there. Or what it did.

"If we do that, will the robot melt or spark or explode or anything like that?" asked Noke, seeing the worry on my cartoon face.

"It'll just be a little jolt to its system," said

Dean. "The robot is probably worn out from doing the waggling dances and silly faces it was famous for. Pressing will just reset its system and maybe make it fresh again. It won't wipe any memories or abilities."

Maybe pressing the button would help. I pointed at my left earhole. *Press it,* I was saying.

Gerry took a small pin that was holding on a toothbrush eyebrow and, letting the eyebrow drop to the floor, handed the pin to Red.

Red carefully put it in my earhole and pressed the button inside.

My face shook. My vision went blue. I could see nothing. Hear nothing.

I *felt* nothing for a moment either.

Nothing at all.

My screen blinked back on and I felt

something again. A little tingle.

Then a *big* tingle. Like a huge wave rising up inside me.

Then, I felt *everything*.

My face glitched through every emotion at once. Happy, sad, worried, confident, angry, calm, afraid, brave. Fighting and shoving and pushing and trying to take over.

It was too much for me.

I backed into the corner and sat on the ground with my hands over my head, hoping it would go away.

"Uh-oh," said Noke.

"0!" said Digits.

"Is everything OK?" I heard Dean ask.

"Perfect!" said Noke. "Not in any way a disaster."

I felt worse than ever.

"You could also try and update your Robot-O-Fun through the internet functions in its face—"

"Great. Thank you. No disasters at all," continued Noke. "I'm a happy human now."

"No problem. Is there anything else I can assist you with today?" asked Dean, cheery again.

"My head keeps falling off," announced Gerry.

"*Your* head keeps falling off?" asked the human.

"And how do we turn off Noke's grumpiness?" added Gerry.

"What …? Sorry, who is this?"

"Humans," said Noke, panicking. "Just humans. We have sponges. In our brains. Bye!"

Noke slapped Gerry's head and the phone went dead.

"5!" said Digits, whose gentle glow bathed me in green.

"I *know* it was a disaster," said Noke. "You don't have to keep saying it."

"How are you feeling, Boot?" asked Red.

"I'm feeling too much!" I shouted.

Red backed away.

"I'm sorry, I didn't mean to shout!" I shouted
again. Then I felt so guilty all of a sudden. "I'm
really upset." My face went blue and cartoon tears
erupted like a fountain on my screen.

"We just need Boot to stay calm," said Red.
"No more excitement."

Gerry's head rang.

Was it Dean the Helpline Man calling back?

Had he realised something was wrong?

Gerry's head kept ringing.

"Don't answer—" said Red.

Gerry answered.

Beth's face appeared as a hologram in the gloomy store room.

I stood quickly, wiped away the cartoon tears from my face and put on a sunny smile like nothing at all was wrong.

"Hi, everyone," said Beth. "Hi, Boot. How are you doing?"

I couldn't tell Beth I was breaking. She was already worried about her grandma. If she knew I was broken too, she would be very upset. I had to keep it a secret. Pretend everything was good. Smile and carry on for her.

"I found a dinosaur," I said.

"A what?" asked Beth, amused by this.

"I found a dinosaur. In Ivy Park. Where you and Grandma used to go. I met Mr Piggles too.

And an octopus. And a hypnotic hamster. And a bear with slippers for claws and ribbons in its fur and …"

I had an idea. I drew on the biggest orange smile even though I felt very broken inside.

"I'll meet you there!"

BETH MEETS THE BRONTOSAURUS

We met the next morning. Beth was in the circle of grass, by the pond, her face lit up by a sliver of sunshine shining through the buildings and her eyes wide as she stood face to face with a pretend brontosaurus.

Sprout's neck rose high with the clacking-clack of turning gears.

Then it lurched sideways, its head banging off the grass

"Wow," said Beth. "That is almost, sort of, like a real dinosaur."

"I like plants," said Sprout, looking up from the ground.

Jordan threw the red ball and Sprout bounded away, tongue hanging out, head dangling backwards.

I stood beside Beth, not even as high as her hip. I was so keen that she like this visit. And that Jordan and Melody like her visit. Maybe they would forget the troubles the park faced, even for a minute. Maybe it would take Beth's mind off her grandma being broken. And maybe it would fix me somehow.

I held Herman the hypno hamster up to her in my palm, almost like a gift, and twirled my cartoon eyes at the same time Herman did.

Beth looked into Herman's deep, irresistible eyes.

"Be careful," said the watching Noke. "Stare at the hamster too long and you'll think you're a chicken."

"*Hee-haw*," said Slippers, having its tummy rubbed by Melody as Mr Piggles, Killer and Poochy bounced around them both.

"Or a donkey!" said Noke. "Hey, maybe that's what happened to the braying bear. Too much time staring at the furball."

"I hope you don't mind me coming here," Beth
said to Jordan.

"Nah, it's good," said Jordan. "It's not our
park. It's meant to be for everyone, it's just no one

really comes in here any more. Too busy with their robots. The wrong type of robots, I mean."

Killer the unicorn bounded by giddily, rainbow colours running through its mane.

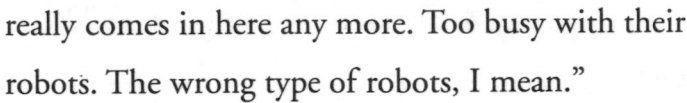

"Did you and your nana come here?" asked Melody, just as Slippers rolled over and almost squashed Mr Piggles.

"Yes," said Beth. "We would sit on that bench over there, the one with the toilet plunger on it."

"Sucky, get off the bench!" said Jordan. The octopus appeared as if by magic, unfurling its tentacles and sliding to the ground and into the pond with a blurt of bubbles.

Beth laughed so hard she had to hold her tummy to stop bursting. Jordan and Melody laughed too. I drew a huge orange smile on my face.

I burped a giggle too. And another. And three more as bubbles of happiness rose inside me.

"Grandma would love this," said Beth when she recovered from the laugh attack. "She used to come here when she was young, before the city was so built up. So she brought me every now and again too. We'd come here and just enjoy the flowers and the birds and the life here."

A butterfly flapped by, rising and falling with each beat of its delicate wings, so light a tiny breath of wind would surely blow it away.

"Butterflies should have bat wings," I said. "The wind wouldn't push them around so much."

Beth, Jordan and Melody looked at me, like this was a very strange idea.

"Bat wings that they could screw on and off," suggested Noke. "Or swap for, like, eagles' wings. You're right, Boot. I wouldn't want to be designed by whoever did the butterfly job."

"I don't know," said Beth. "I think nature's pretty amazing. Figuring out how to fly, how to swim—"

Killer the unicorn bounded by on four stiff legs.

"How to walk," she smiled.

"Yeah," said Jordan. "Like an octopus's camouflage – a real one, I mean. That stuff's incredible."

"Or how an apple seed makes a new tree," said Beth, picking up a loose apple from the ground.

"When you think about it—"

"Which I don't," said Noke, grumpy.

"—these are the most incredible machines ever. Millions of years to be made. Without any instructions."

She stopped talking to take it all in, so we did the same. Even Poochy, Mr Piggles and Slippers lay still, on their backs, for a moment.

A bright yellow butterfly flew across my vision, almost like a leaf on the breeze. It landed on my face, and I crossed my cartoon eyes for a proper look.

The butterfly wafted its wings twice and flew off again, surfing the tiny breeze.

I went to reach for it and wobbled awkwardly forward.

It became clear to me all of a sudden.

The robots here, we did a lot of things *like* humans or animals. We walked *like* humans or animals. We talked *like* humans but we had the electronic edge to our voices.

The way we made a little whirring noise or glitched when we said *ruff*.

The way we ran – or couldn't run.

Nothing made in a factory could ever be as amazing as the life here – human or animal or plant.

"The park. It's …" I looked for the word in my head full of many words. "… another big surprise to me."

"Oink," said Mr Piggles. An earwig sat on the pig's snout, the pincers on its tail opening and closing lazily.

I'd thought I knew so much, but now I suddenly had many questions.

"How are insects so small yet so powerful?" I asked. "Why are there so many greens?"

"You're funny," said Melody.

"Why are toes shaped like toes? How are butterflies really just grown-up caterpillars?"

"You'll burn your brain circuits out if you keep asking questions," said Noke.

"It's awesome," said Beth. "And so sad that someone would want to destroy this. Do you know who sent the ground-bot?"

Jordan shook his head.

"Bad people," said Melody. "Silly people."

"If people just stopped looking at the screens on their robots," said Jordan. "Just for a short while. All this is, like, right here in front of them, but they walk past it. They don't even see it."

"I'm so glad you brought me back here," Beth said to me.

She ran her fingers across the slats of the bench, as if that would help make the memory of sitting there with her grandma real.

I had an idea.

"Would you like to see Grandma here again?" I asked eagerly, my voice rising higher.

"I would love that more than anything, Boot, but I'm not sure it can be done. It's too hard for her to leave the elderly care home."

"But I remember it," I said. "I have my hologram of the memory. It won't be the same, but if you allow me I can show it to you."

Beth looked up at the sky and then back around at the buildings. For a moment her eyes focussed on the great advertising screen looking over the park. An ad for perfume was followed by the ad for the coffee shops again. That same woman, her ice-white hair cutting across half her face, as she lifted the cup and winked.

I knew Beth was letting her brain work out what she would like and maybe what she would be able to see without getting upset.

"That would be nice," she said after 6.102 seconds.

I felt so happy I thought I might crack right down the middle.

I pushed my belly upwards to make sure things would look right, and found the memory deep within.

The light in my belly winked on and slowly, carefully, I brought the hologram of Grandma into the day. Grandma from before she was sick. Before she changed. Before I changed too.

Grandma sat on the bench, a see-through picture, yet as real as if she had walked into the park just a minute ago. Moving. Smiling. Happy. Enjoying the breeze and the butterflies and the flowers and so many greens it was impossible to count them all.

This is how Grandma was on the last day I came here. Before both of us became a bit broken.

"Oh …" said Beth, "… wow."

"Maybe we should leave you to it," said Jordan, turning away.

"No," said Beth, beckoning him to stay. "It's OK. This is your park. It's *everybody's* park. I want you to see how happy Grandma was here."

In this memory Grandma looked up across the green, almost as if she was looking at us. Her smile

was strong, like this was a place she could sit in for ever.

Beth moved to the bench and sat beside Grandma, sliding up right beside her. She carefully placed her hand on Grandma's. Of course, Grandma wasn't really there – and Beth couldn't really touch her hand – but she let hers hover over it as if it was all real.

"Thank you, Boot," she said, while still looking at Grandma's smiling face. "Maybe we'll be able to bring Grandma back here some day, before …" Beth took a shallow breath. "Before it's too late. You can let her go now."

I turned off the hologram, slowly letting it fade until the space on the bench where Grandma had been was empty.

"Thank you," Beth said again and everyone stayed silent so as not to spoil the moment.

But inside, I was not silent. My voice was telling me to shout.

I should have felt happy about this. I should still have felt joy, like I had done something good.

I didn't.

I felt something completely different.

I felt upset. No, I felt angry. Angry that Beth couldn't come here with Grandma now. That Grandma was broken and couldn't just be fixed. And that made me remember that I was broken and wasn't fixed. And then I wondered if showing Grandma on the bench would make Beth sad and angry too. And that made me more angry.

And the angriness wanted to take over everything now.

"Boot," said Noke.

"What?" I snapped at Noke. I didn't mean to snap.

"Your face."

I looked into the pond. Below the surface I could see the shadow of a robot octopus. But I could see my reflection in the ripples. My screen –

my face – was turning an even deeper shade of red.

"Are you OK?" asked Noke.

I was not OK. Something was wrong. Very wrong.

I concentrated hard to get the redness in my face to go away before I could look at Beth again.

I wanted to tell her something was wrong. That I was broken again. That nothing could fix it.

My cartoon mouth opened but I couldn't say anything.

I didn't get a chance to anyway, because Jordan shouted a sudden warning to the pets.

"Hide, everyone. Someone's coming!"

C☗FFEE W☗MAN

"Get back into the bushes to be safe," said Jordan, guiding the robot pets into a large hollow hidden in the branches and leaves.

Sprout the brontosaurus bashed and crashed about a bit until Melody had an idea and threw a fallen apple into the bushes. As if the apple was a ball, the robot dinosaur bounded in after it, snapping twigs as it dragged its long neck and curved tail out of view.

Noke and I quickly retreated behind the trees and bushes too, Beth giving a thumbs-up when she was sure we were OK.

From behind the thick branches and large glossy leaves I saw a woman approach from around the bend in the path, short but hurried steps taking her towards the circle of grass.

It was the woman I had met when running

away from the park yesterday. Coffee Woman.
In fact, she had a coffee again, holding it in two
hands to keep it – or herself – warm. She wore a
long dark coat, buttoned up to her neck, and her
hat pulled tightly over her head.

"Your face is still bright red," Noke said to me
as quietly as possible. "You need to calm down
before you go *kaboom*."

Noke snapped a wide, thick leaf off a plant
growing tall beside us and held it over my screen.

"Stop," I told Noke, annoyed.

"Excuse me?" Coffee Woman said to Jordan as
she arrived. She must have heard me speak.

"He said don't … don't … don't *stop* just
because we're here," stuttered Beth. "The bench is
free."

"Thank you," she said, sitting exactly where the
hologram memory of Grandma had been only a
minute before.

Picking a flake of old paint from the bench, she

sipped her coffee while looking around at the park.

"So you kids play here?" she asked quickly, like she just had to get the words out.

"Yep," said Melody. "It's our garden."

Coffee Woman smiled and sipped before letting more words tumble out. "It is a wonderful spot to have coffee."

Noke leaned in and whispered to me. "Too much

coffee makes humans all jittery and speeded up, like they've got a bolt of electricity to their heads."

Coffee Woman stood again and walked along the path, past the shadows of the robots in the bushes.

"We like it here," said Jordan.

"Me too. Some day soon, maybe the whole city will learn to enjoy this place," she said, drinking more coffee. "Wouldn't that be nice?"

"Yep," said Melody, smiling.

"It's such a perfect place," she said, the words almost tumbling out from her mouth. "I wish the whole world would drink their coffee here, just like me." After another sip from her cup, she lifted it as if to say *cheers* as humans do and walked out of sight.

"Coast's clear," said Jordan. Herman the hypno hamster's wide eyes and whiskers popped out through a shrub.

Killer bounced out of the undergrowth with a flower stuck at the top of its horn. Poochy and Mr Piggles resumed their tumbles and twists. Sprout just stayed in the hollow, neck resting on the tree trunk, apple in its mouth.

It was time for Beth to go. She touched the jewel on my chest and after a goodbye hug that made me feel warm – but not explodey warm – she looked around at Ivy Park before turning to Melody and Jordan.

"This place is precious. I can see it. That

woman with the coffee said it too. I'm sure no one will let this park be torn down. Not while it has you two looking after it. *And* looking after the dinosaurs and unicorns and a hamster so really, really cute that I kind of want to eat it all up."

"Eating a robot hamster would break your teeth," I said, because I didn't want that to happen to Beth. I also didn't want Herman to get eaten.

Smiling, she gave me a pat on the head. "Don't ever change, Boot."

After Beth left, Melody played with the pets and Jordan tried to find a way to calm down the over-excited Killer.

Noke and I sat on the bench.

"You didn't tell Beth you're broken," said Noke. "She could help get you fixed."

"No," I said, snapping again. "I don't want to make her worry any more about anything."

"What's wrong with you?" asked Jordan, concerned.

"Boot is not working properly," said Noke.

"Oh, like how?" asked Jordan.

"Up and down," said Noke.

"A bit like Killer, then," said Jordan, trying to calm the giddy unicorn. "Melody, did you fiddle with Killer's buttons again?"

His sister immediately got upset.

"I did not!" she said. "You always say that to me. *Stop* saying that."

"OK, sorry."

"Stop blaming me for Killer being crazy. I'd never hurt Killer."

Melody was very upset. Her face went a bit red. Just like mine.

A breath of a breeze ran through the park.

Noke sighed an electronic sigh. "That's nice. The fresh air helps blow the dust from my ears. I'm not joking. Dusty ears are a big problem. If the dust gets into my brain, I'm fried. Nothing smells worse than fried robot brains."

This made Melody laugh, which surprised me because Melody had been very angry only a few seconds before. Happy again, she petted Herman while humming gently.

Noke examined my head. "There's no smoke coming from you, so it mustn't be fried brains. Your problem must be from something else."

On the giant screen, an ad ran for one of the sophisticated robots everyone already had, sleek with their domed heads and amazing abilities.

UPDATE YOUR ROBOT TODAY!

said the ad.

JUST LOG ON TO THE INTERNET TO GET NEW SKILLS AND FIX OLD PROBLEMS.

Noke's face lifted with a creak. This always meant Noke had an idea. "That's it. We should try the update. That's what Helpline Man said."

"I don't want any more—"

"—disaster?" guessed Noke correctly. "You mightn't have noticed, Boot, but things aren't exactly going not-disastrous for you right now. So let's find a quiet corner and see if we can give you a boost."

SUPERB**OO**T

Noke and I found a sheltered hollow in the corner of the park, surrounded by gnarled branches and scattered with crumpled drinks cans.

"Is an update safe?" I asked.

"Most robots need one every now and again," said Noke. "It helps them work faster or to get new skills and fixes things when they go wrong."

"*I'm* going wrong," I said.

"The advert on the big screen said that all you have to do is go on to the internet. Can you do that by just thinking about it?"

I thought about going on the internet. Really concentrated on it, with my cartoon eyes squeezed tight and a bead of cartoon sweat running down my face. But I didn't feel any different. I didn't feel like I was connected to anything except my own worried thoughts and the cracked feeling in my tummy.

"OK, let's try something different," said Noke, lifting a chunky finger. "Do you remember what Helpline Man said? You can access the internet through your face."

Yes, I had a memory from before I woke up – before I became *me* – of Beth's mother prodding my face, then swiping across. Her tongue stuck out of the side of her mouth as she concentrated on finding what she wanted.

"How did you change the language settings so the robot only speaks Chinese?" she was asking a young Beth, fretting behind her.

Noke waggled the chunky finger over my face. "I've been on the streets a while. I've fixed up a few things in that time. You can trust me."

"Be careful, Noke," I said.

Staring into my face, Noke blocked out my view of everything else and began prodding and swiping across my screen. I didn't like having someone just prod me like this.

"Stand still. My fingers are a bit clumsy for this." Noke poked and swiped and pushed. "Why do humans make things so badly?"

"That doesn't make me feel better, Noke …"

"Oh, look, I've found a way to turn your volume up and down." Noke began to do that.

"Please don't make my voice go quiet. I … and really would like to be heard. Thank you."

Noke prodded and swiped some more.

"Right, here's the function I've been looking for. It says to **LOG ON TO WIFI AND CHECK FOR UPDATES.** I just need to swipe here …" Noke swiped there. "… and press there …" Noke pressed there.

"Is this going to be safe?" I asked.

"Perfectly safe. As long as you don't get a computer virus."

"A computer virus?" I asked, eyes wide on my screen.

"Yeah, that would be *terrible*. A bit like the Wipes, only 417 times worse. But, you know, I'm sure that won't happen as long as I press the right thing here. Oh, hold on, I've lost it. Where is it? Is it this bit?"

"Be careful, Noke."

"Found it," said Noke. "I'll just press this and you'll go online … *Now*."

My screen flickered.

My mind flickered.

Then very little happened.

Just a tingle through my circuits. A tiny tickle of my brain.

"Sorry, Noke, but I don't think anything's happen— **UPDATING**," I suddenly announced without meaning to. **"PLEASE STAND BY."**

Even though I didn't *go* anywhere I felt like my mind was rushing through a tunnel at 5,000 miles an hour.

A multi-coloured tunnel.

A multi-coloured tunnel made of information and ideas and skills, with smaller tunnels shooting off in all directions. It was so much information. *Too* much information.

This was the internet.

My mind was in it, even though my body was still in the park. It was like being in two places at once.

No, it was like being *everywhere* at once.

I was part of computers in nearby buildings.

I was part of the robots on the city streets.

I was in the cars driving past and drones

flying above.

I was in computer games, building houses and blasting baddies.

I was in music.

I was in drawings.

I was in movies and cartoons and words and pictures.

I was even in the big advertising screen overlooking the park.

I could look down from it and see Noke standing beside me, even though I was also all the way up here. Noke was looking back up at the screen.

"Boot, I just saw your face on that screen," Noke said, sounding very far away from me. "Just for a quarter of a second, but it was there. How did you do that?"

Before I could answer I was sucked back through the tunnel again.

Away from the screen and the drones and cars and robots and every computer.

Sucked back through the multi-coloured tunnel, passing a blur of information and ideas and voices and pictures.

Until my mind crashed back into my own head.

I slumped to the ground.

"Whoah," I said.

That was the only word I could find to describe it.

I knew *new* things. Skills. Out of nowhere. As if I'd always known them.

UPDATE COMPLETE blinked on my screen.

My screen flickered. My cartoon eyes opened. I looked at Noke.

"I know juggling," I said.

"Show me," said Noke, finding a pine cone and old tennis ball in the bushes and handing them to me. Looking for a third object, Noke picked up a snail. The snail didn't look like it wanted to be juggled.

But I juggled. I juggled brilliantly.

"Woo-hoo," said Noke, impressed.

I threw the snail high in the air, held the tennis ball and pine cone, did a spin, caught the snail and went "ta-dah".

I hadn't wanted to say "ta-dah".

"That was *great!*" said Noke. "What else can you do?"

Noke tapped my face.

"Please don't do that," I said. "I might have learned dangerous ninja skills."

Noke stepped back warily, but quickly decided I didn't know ninja skills and started tapping my face again.

"You have loads of new skills," said Noke. "There's a list of them on your screen. Let's try Pirate Mode."

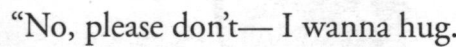

"Noke, I don't think you should— Arrr, begone me landlubbing hearty or I'll keelhaul every man jack of you! Arrr."

"Brilliant," said Noke, amused.

"Arrrr!" I said, unamused.

"And now Toddler Mode," said Noke.

"No, please don't— I wanna hug. Boo boo, bah bah. Hee-hee." I toddled around in a circle. "Me your best friend. I have a boo boo on my bum bum."

"Oh, this is gold," said Noke, stopping me and scrolling through my screen for more things.

"Boot no like. I go cry cry," I said.

"Monkey Mode," said Noke.

"Oooh-aaah," I said, with my arms pulled up under my armpits. I scratched the top of my head. "Oooh-oooh-aah-aaah. Banana."

"Oh, here's one that might help. Healthy Mode."

I stopped acting like a monkey and a little chef's hat popped up on my screen. "It's fun to eat vegetables! Tomatoes are fruit, you know! Celery is cool!"

"Celery is cool? Oh dear," said Noke, pressing my screen one final time.

I whistled so loudly a squirrel fell off a nearby tree.

"OK, we don't like the whistling," said Noke. "You know something, Boot? I think I liked you just the way you were."

I felt a blast of relief as Noke pressed the mode that put me back to normal. But that feeling lasted only a few seconds.

"Is your problem fixed, Boot?" asked Noke.

I listened to my body. To my mind. Tried to hear past the quiet whirr of machinery and little creaks of my plastic body. To feel what might be in there. To see if the broken part was still there.

It was.

I knew it.

I knew the crack must be there because I felt like shouting. I felt like shouting really, really loudly. And screaming. And pushing. And shoving. And telling everyone in the whole world to go away and leave me alone.

But I didn't shout.

Someone else did.

It was Melody, and she was screaming.

THE PARK IN DANGER

"An earthquake made my tooth fall out."

Melody held up a small white tooth. Gulping down a sob, she pulled back the corner of her mouth to show a gap where it had been. She leaked from her eyes and her nose while Jordan bent down and locked eyes with her.

"An earthquake?" said Jordan. "Made your tooth fall out?"

"Yep. My tooth was wobbly already, though," sniffled Melody.

"Are you *sure* it was an earthquake?" asked Jordan.

Melody fixed Jordan with such a strong glare I wondered if laser beams might shoot out of the little girl's eyes even though little girls didn't shoot laser beams out of their eyes. At least, I thought I knew that. Maybe I was about to find out.

There was a rumble through the ground.

"See!" said Melody. "Earthquake!"

I felt a rumble through my egg-shaped legs into my round belly, all the way up to my head.

Noke's eyebrows creaked. Mr Piggles's snout jangled. The unicorn missed a bounce and landed horn-first in the grass.

Sprout stuck its neck out for a look, and it swayed before flopping to the ground.

The robot pets began to make noise. They *oink*ed and *miaow*ed and *bark*ed and *rahr*ed and *hee-haw*ed.

"The water's jumping around," said Melody, pointing at the pond.

The pond rippled and then sloshed like a basin of water. Sucky the octopus appeared on the surface, flickering in confusion.

"Is something in the water with Sucky?" I asked, as a great bubble rose through the slime-green pond. Reaching the surface, it popped with a greasy *bleurp*.

Sucky's eyes blinked and turned to see what was happening.

More bubbles came, one after another, each popping on the surface with a sound that reminded me of when Beth's dad tried to keep a burp down after a heavy dinner.

Bleurrb.
Bleurrb.
Gurgle.

"That's not good," said Noke.

The pond began to drain away, the water swirling towards the middle.

All too quickly, Sucky was sitting on damp, sludgy concrete. Small stranded fish flopped all around a wide hole through which the water had gone.

The ground-bot's periscope pushed up through the hole in the ground, looked around, saw Sucky's suckers about to slap down on it and *meep-meep*ed before disappearing back underground again.

Everything was quiet for a moment.

Even the birds had gone silent.

But the rumbling grew through the ground. A tremble from something close.

Sprout the brontosaurus tried to keep its head steady, but it swayed and dipped, a wave rippling through its neck with a clickity-clack.

"Wait here," said Jordan, sprinting off towards the front of the park.

"Whatever it is, it's big," said Noke.

I put my hand on the ground and could feel the low thrum of something through the soil, up my arm, through my head. I lifted my hand away in case it made my broken insides worse.

A worm pushed from under the grass, wriggling

awkwardly until it flopped on to the surface with blobs of soil along its body. More worms followed, slowly emerging from below the grass. Something was forcing them up.

"This is really scary," said Melody and her face wobbled, very like mine did. She hugged Slippers, whose back fur still had some ribbons tied in it.

Herman Hamster popped up from her pocket, squeezed between the two of them.

"I want Jordan back," said Melody, hugging tighter.

I wanted Jordan back too. I wanted the earthquakes to stop and the ground to be normal again.

And more than any of this I wanted Melody to feel better. I wanted to burp a giggle. To dance. To waggle. To do a trick. To make her happy.

There wasn't time.

Through the rumbling we heard fast footsteps getting closer. Jordan arrived, jumping awkwardly over loose branches. He was out of breath and sounding very alarmed.

"Bulldozerbots! … Diggers! …. Outside! …" gasped Jordan. "They're about to tear down the park!"

BULLD☉ZERB☉TS

We crept carefully along the curving path until we could see the park gates. I stayed two steps behind Jordan and Noke, and half a step behind Melody and Slippers.

There were some people in bright yellow jackets and helmets, and they'd taped off the front of the park – criss-cross tape that had 'DANGER DEMOLITION!' written on it.

Just inside the park, their engines already revving, were two huge vehicles. At the front of each was a large sharp blade, glinting in the sunlight and ready to start tearing up the ground.

The engines juddered so loudly it felt like my head might rattle off.

"Why?" asked Melody, and this time she wasn't crying but seemed stunned – as if the surprise and shock had knocked all the tears away.

"I don't know," said Jordan. "All I know is that we have to stop them. This is the last bit of green in the city. We can't lose this too."

"We could show them Herman," said Melody. "No one could bulldoze Herman."

Herman looked up out of her pocket, eyes bright, blue and swirling.

"I don't know, Melody. If they don't care about the life and nature in this park, then why will they care about robots?" Jordan looked at Noke and me. "Sorry."

"Unusually for a human, you're making sense," said Noke, whose right shoulder was being shaken by the trembling of the bulldozerbots. "They'll turn us all into bits no bigger than human brains. Which are *tiny*." Noke looked at Jordan and Melody. "Sorry."

The trembling felt like it was getting more and more intense. I held the crack on my face to stop it getting wider but knew there wasn't much I could do to stop my insides from breaking.

One of the humans at the front of the park looked around and, squinting with hands up over his eyes, spotted us. He slapped the arm of the man standing beside him and pointed in our direction.

"Hey, kids!" he shouted.

"Let's go!"

said Jordan and we scrambled back to where the pets were gathered already, waiting for us as if expecting orders.

Sucky was flashing in and out of camouflage as if not sure what to do without water.

Slippers paced slowly in a circle. *Thud ... flump.*

"We have to save this place," said Jordan, holding Melody's hand to calm her. "It's too special to just be dug up. This is all that's left. This is all *we* have left. We need a plan. Now."

I felt that fire in my belly. A tummy ache.

"We could run," said Noke. "Running would be good. And it is not a chicken plan. It's a don't-get-torn-apart plan."

The rumbling through the park shook the leaves, scared off the birds, jolted flecks of paint from the bench, made Sprout's head wobble and Mr Piggles's snout shake.

A squirrel darted down a tree behind me, and I

turned at the sudden noise. But I saw something else. Through the bushes. On the street. A sweep of movement on the other side.

An arm lifting. A hand raising a cup.

A woman sipping it.

Coffee Woman.

I had an idea. A lightbulb appeared on my face to tell everyone else.

I thought about what I needed to do.

Searched for the power inside me.

And I let out the loudest whistle I could to get Coffee Woman's attention.

Birds scattered. Jordan and Melody grabbed their ears. Noke's eyebrows almost fell off in surprise. Killer fell over and landed horn-first in the grass.

Coffee Woman looked around, confused for a moment, before swivelling about and putting her face into a tiny gap in the trees.

"What on earth is going on?"

B⚙⚙T'S BIG IDEA

Coffee Woman disappeared again.

We heard the *click-clack* of her shoes as she walked hurriedly away.

The bulldozerbots sat idle. Their engines ran but they didn't get any closer, any louder. There was no sound of digging or churning or tearing.

Just a terrible wait.

"Do you hear footsteps?" asked Jordan.

The *click-clacks* were back. She had come to help us.

"Go," Melody said, starting to usher the pets towards their hiding place. "Bushes. Hurry."

"Get in the bushes. Get out of the bushes. Get back into the bushes," complained Noke, lifting Sprout's flopping head to help it go faster. "We're the ones who have to stay out of the way, even when it's the humans causing all the trouble."

"**RUFFF**," said Poochy, somersaulting on to the leaves. "**RUFFFSSSPPTTT**."

"I will stay," I said to Melody, eager even as every wire in my body was filled with worry. "I whistled for her. I can show her what will happen. With my face. Then she will help us."

"We can't let her know you're … you're *you*," said Jordan.

"I will play dumb," I said.

"I'm beginning to think you're all playing dumb," said Noke, following Sprout over a low branch and out of sight.

We watched as a shadow approached from the main part of the park. It stretched along the path until the woman appeared, her hands wrapped around a coffee cup as always.

"I did not expect to see you again so soon," she said to Jordan and Melody, as if it was just a normal day in a normal park that was not about to be torn up.

"Uh, hi?" replied Jordan. "Again."

Melody lifted me in the crook of her arm, just like I was a toy. Like Beth used to do. I rested there, against her shoulder, blank for now, trying to tell my tummy ache to go away.

The woman walked to the centre of the grass and slowly looked around. She took a sip from her coffee, walked to the bench and sat on it. Just like she had done before.

"You shouldn't be here," she said, quickly.

The ground shivered under the engines of the bulldozerbots. The butterflies and bees rose like a small cloud from the flowers. Some red apples fell from the tree, bouncing on the grass.

There was a rustle in the bushes, and I guessed it was Sprout eager to play fetch.

"They're tearing this place down," said Jordan.

"Our garden," said Melody, sniffling and hugging me. "Will be gone."

She held me forward and I drew the bulldozerbots for Coffee Woman. I drew cartoon monsters munching up cartoon trees. I drew butterflies and bees and squirrels and a unicorn, all being chased away, with cartoon skyscrapers rising in their place.

"Is this your toy?" she asked Melody.

Melody nodded.

"I met it yesterday when I was here," said Coffee Woman. "It was almost like it was running away. It bumped into me. It was almost as if the little thing was alive."

She laughed briefly and tickled under my chin before taking a sip of coffee. "It's cracked. And dirty. And its hip has a hole in it. You should get your money back on it. Get a new one. It's always good to have something new."

She blew the thin wisp of steam escaping through the lid of her coffee cup.

It fogged up my screen for a second.

An apple dropped from the tree and again I could hear Sprout shift in the bushes.

Coffee Woman looked that way.

"You passed the bulldozers, yeah?" Jordan asked her. "Did you talk to the men there?"

"Oh yes," she said, her attention back on us. "A café is going to be built here."

"*Another* café?" asked Jordan. "There's already one just up the street and another just down that direction. But there's only one park left."

Coffee Woman looked at her coffee with its picture of the sideways triangle on it. The symbol that had once brought me to Beth.

"People like coffee," she said.

The huge screen on the building above flashed images, unnatural colours intruding on Ivy Park's greens. All the things people were supposed to buy.

"We have to stop them," said Melody.

"Right," said Coffee Woman.

"They won't care about what we say," said

Jordan, pleading now. "They'll think we're just kids. But you're a grown-up. You come here every day. Maybe they'll listen to you. Can you help us?"

A chill breeze ran through the air.

"Oh yes, they will listen to me all right," Coffee Woman said. "I could stop this, no doubt about it."

I saw relief fill Jordan and Melody's faces. A hopeful smile from Jordan.

Melody wiped her nose with the back of her arm.

An apple dropped from the tree. A red, knobbly apple bobbling to a stop at Coffee Woman's feet.

She saw it, picked it up and examined it for a second before tossing it away.

Sprout burst from the trees, head flopping about wildly, bounding across the grass to grab the apple.

Coffee Woman didn't have time to duck fully as Sprout's long neck whipped towards her, its head

knocking her hat clean off so it flew across the
grass.

With me dangling from one hand, Melody
went to grab Sprout. Jordan dashed to help Coffee
Woman, who was turned away, one hand over her
head.

"Are you OK?" asked Jordan. "So sorry about
that. It's a broken robot. It didn't mean …"

She turned. Sat up straight again, revealing her hair for the first time.

"Oh no," said Jordan, looking at her and then over her shoulder.

Oh no?

Then I understood.

On the giant screen, the ad for the café had appeared again. With the familiar logo. And a smiling woman, ice-white hair, winking and lifting the cup to her mouth, a welcoming smile crossing her lips.

It was her. It was Coffee Woman.

Here, in the park in front of us, she held up the coffee. But she didn't wink. She didn't smile.

"You," said Jordan. "*You're* knocking our park down."

C☼FFEE TIME

The bulldozerbot engines sent a shudder through the trees, shook leaves loose, forced the last birds to fly to safety.

I imagined their jaws wide open, eager to start ripping the park apart.

Hanging from Melody's hand, I saw everything from a strange angle, and it felt like the world was turning upside down. I'd thought I could help. I had only brought more trouble.

My ache grew achier.

I was truly broken.

"You said you'd help us stop them?" asked Jordan.

"No," said Coffee Woman. "I said I *could* stop them. I didn't say I *would*. And now that I see there's so much broken and dangerous rubbish around this place, I reckon I'm doing you and everyone a favour getting rid of this park before it gets worse."

Spying something on the ground, she bent carefully to pick it up.

It was a bow. A pink bow. It had a little tuft of bear fur on it. She dropped it and began to walk away.

"Don't ruin our garden," Melody asked, stunned.

"I am not ruining anything," Coffee Woman said, sounding insulted by the accusation. "I am *building* something. Something great. Something everyone can use. I mean, look at this place now. You're the only ones I ever see in here. You and some dumb machines."

She marched towards Jordan, forcing him to take a step back. "In fact, we're standing right where there'll be a row of coffee machines and cakes of every colour. And where you are standing, little girl …"

Coffee Woman took a couple of steps towards Melody, who bolted behind Jordan, while I flopped about trying to stay toy-like – which was easy now I felt broken.

"… This is where we'll have lovely seats. Orange seats, like our sign. The brightest orange we can find. And over there by that apple tree is where the toilets will be."

She walked to the empty pond, gesturing with her coffee. "And here at this big muddy puddle, with the toilet plunger and a vacuum cleaner hose thrown in it, will be the counter where thousands of people will come every day to pay for *my* coffee from *my* shop. And all that means one thing should be very clear. It's not your garden. It's *mine*."

Angry, she gripped her coffee cup so tight it released a splash of coffee through the lid.

"Why do this?" asked Jordan.

She responded like it was the strangest question

in the whole world. "Why would I not? Yes, there is a café up the street there." She pointed left, then right. "And one up the street that way." She pointed at the ground. "But there is no café *here*."

The coffee splashed again. I noticed she had gripped the cup so tightly her knuckles were white and she looked like she might crush it completely.

"But the park …" said Melody, lifting me in the crook of her arm.

"There is plenty of this world left for leaves and twigs and insects and rubbish in ponds," the woman said. "We'll have plants in our shop. Sure, they'll be plastic plants, but no one will care. People only care about their morning coffee. People only care about stuffing their faces with cakes. They only care about eating and drinking and spending money. Why should they care about *this*? There's plenty of grass out there somewhere …"

She waved in a general direction, splashing the coffee again.

"But … we have pets," said Melody meekly.

Coffee Woman checked her watch, then looked back towards the unseen bulldozerbots and the wrecking crew. "If they want animals they can see them on the internet or in the zoo or they can buy pretend ones and throw them out when they're bored."

"You're wrong," said Jordan, standing tall. "People care."

"When you grow up, you'll learn one very important lesson in life. People. Are. Idiots," hissed Coffee Woman. "Idiots! They don't care about anything but looking at screens and spending money. People wouldn't even notice your precious park is gone unless someone puts it on a screen for them."

I felt the ache in me go from my tummy into my legs to my head, every wire, every piece of me.

"Now, you children can leave by the front gate, or through that gap in the hedge over there. I thought the bulldozerbots would have frightened you off by now. Anyway, whichever way you choose to leave, it's time to go. I have a café to build."

She lifted her hand and realised that milky coffee had dripped down her sleeve. Irritated, she threw the cup away. It lay in the bushes, lid half off, coffee pouring over beautiful purple flowers.

Pulling a napkin from her coat pocket, she carefully dried her hands.

"You can't do this," said Jordan.

Coffee Woman walked to the turn in the path where she could see the machines waiting to destroy the park. She lifted the coffee-stained napkin before bringing it down in a swoosh.

"Bulldozerbots," she called out. "Go to work."

ATTACK ☼F THE BULLD☼ZERB☼TS

Coffee Woman left. In her place came a terrible noise.

SPRUNCHHHH!

"Was that a *sprunch*?" asked Noke, head appearing through the undergrowth.

CRRUNNNKKKK!

"That was *definitely* a *crunk*," said Noke, arriving by our sides with a twig stuck in one ear.

The leaves of the highest trees in the gardens wobbled. They shook. Birds that had settled during the brief calm scattered again.

SPRUNNCCHHH!

CRUNNKKK!

The bulldozerbots were moving in.

I was broken. And useless now.

Maybe all my insides would just be shaken apart.

We gathered at the edge of the path, trying to figure out a plan.

"We are *not* leaving," said Jordan.

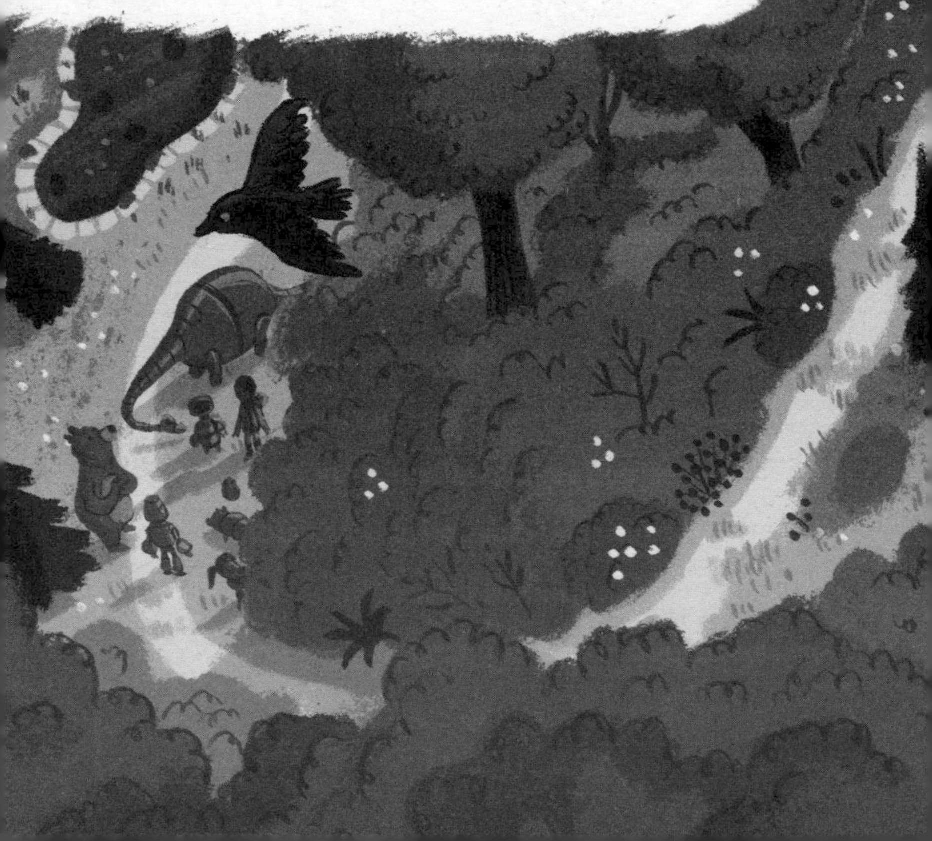

The bulldozerbot rumbled slowly through the park towards us, its wide blade glinting in the light. It was followed by a second, its blade just as sharp.

"We'll all get turned into coffee grinders if we don't run," said Noke.

"I don't want this,"said Melody.

My cartoon face dimmed, all colour leaving it so my eyes and mouth were just grey against a blank screen. I felt every part of me was broken now, like I was almost totally run down. I could hardly make my legs move. My arms were weighed down by my side. I looked at Melody, one cheek wet with tears and the other pressed into Slippers's fur. I knew how she felt.

"*Hee-haw,*" said Slippers, to make her feel better.

I had enough energy to shake my head a little. "I wish I could do something, but I tried and it didn't work because I am very broken now."

"Can you help, Noke?" asked Jordan.

"I know I'm mostly indestructible, but those bulldozerbots will turn me into tinsel in seconds. How can I stay and let that happen?"

Jordan thought for a moment, then something

seemed to cross his mind. "That woman said you robots were … what was it? Oh yeah, dumb machines. But I guess you don't care about proving her wrong."

Noke's face squeaked into a look of pure determination. "Noke's Rules of the Street no. 99. No sponge-for-brains – no offence to you two sponges-for-brains – will ever insult me and get away with it. I am no robot chicken. Count me in."

The noise of the approaching bulldozerbots made my head rattle.

It made Noke's shoulders shudder.

It made Melody cling tighter to Jordan's hand.

Squatting to address me, Jordan said, "Boot, you take Melody and hide behind the bench. Your job is to mind her. If it gets too dangerous, escape through the railings behind the hedges and get on to the street. But it won't come to that, because I have an idea. Actually, it's Melody's idea."

She looked at him, uncertain.

"We'll use the pets, just like you said."

Melody liked this, clapping her hands twice until the rumble of the bulldozerbots sent a tremor through the ground so strong we almost fell over.

"Noke, you take Slippers into the bushes over there—" said Jordan.

"How did I know this plan would involve robots hiding in bushes?" said Noke.

"— and when I give the signal, send the big bear out to say hello."

We found our place behind the bench, ready to watch from through the flaking slats. Mr Piggles, Poochy and Killer rolled and bounded over to the ground behind us with the usual giddiness, like nothing was wrong.

I tried to cheer up Melody by lighting up my face and putting on a bright sunny, orange smile. But I couldn't get the smile right and its colour was a dirty brown.

Melody's look told me she was almost as scared

by my face as she was by the bulldozerbots.

"Sorry," I said, hunching, my head dropping. "I am so broken."

"That's how I feel too," said Melody, and she gave me a hug. It felt good.

The two bulldozerbots interrupted, rumbling around the edges that blocked off our part of the

park, clipping twigs, tearing branches, smushing flowers and leaving ridged tyre tracks in the grass. One after the other, they invaded.

From behind a bush on the other side of the grass circle, Noke pointed towards the muddy, drained pond where Jordan had crouched low and almost out of view.

There was no sign of Sucky the octopus.

The bulldozerbots spread out, side by side, and lowered their blades until they were wedged in the surface of the grass, ready to move forward and tear up everything in their paths.

They lurched forward.

And stopped.

The machines lurched again, their wheels

spinning on the ground, spitting up grass, dirt and earthworms. But still, they were stuck. What could be stopping them moving?

"What's going on?" asked a construction worker in an orange coat and white helmet, striding towards the bulldozerbots, boots squelching on the muddy tracks they'd left behind. "Hey, Mac, we have a problem with these bulldozerbots."

A second worker followed, pushing back his helmet to scratch his forehead.

"They should be working fine, Dave," said Mac. "I checked them all myself this morning. Gave their blades a fresh sharpen and all."

"Well, Mac, they're stuck here," said Dave. "And I don't want to explain it to the boss or she'll squish us like one of those cream buns she has in her cafés."

"They're very nice cream buns, though," said Mac, examining the tracks of a stuck bulldozerbot.

"Tasty all right," said Dave, inspecting another bulldozerbot.

"See anything?" asked Mac.

"Nope," said Dave. "Just this bit of vacuum cleaner with a toilet plunger on it that seems to be sort of hovering here for some reason."

It was Sucky! All but invisible to the two men, the robot octopus had stuck its tentacles to the

172

bulldozers and was holding them in its firm immovable grip.

"I'll shut the machines off for a moment and have a look in their engines," said Dave.

Jordan crept up to the bench, crouching down behind us. "OK, time for another distraction."

Half-standing, Jordan whistled so loudly it made the eyes on my screen wobble. In the trees opposite, Noke urged Slippers into the open. The robot bear lumbered forward, *thud-flump-thudding* up behind Mac the construction worker so quickly that by the time the man turned to face him, Slippers was already looking over him, teeth bared.

"B ..." said Mac, frozen to the spot with fear. "B ..."

Too busy checking the stuck bulldozerbots, Dave didn't look up at first.

"B ... B ..." stuttered Mac.

"What are you jabbering on about?" asked

Dave, looking up and seeing Slippers standing threateningly over Mac. "Bear ..." he gasped.

"And now the secret weapon," said Jordan with a confident smile. Removing fluffy Herman from his pocket, he pointed the hamster in the direction of the construction workers.

Herman scampered away from us, across the grass, under the stuck bulldozerbots, around the feet of the frightened Mac and stopped right in front of Dave.

"What the ..." said Dave, stooping to pick up the pretend hamster. He held Herman up and was immediately hypnotised by the hamster's enormous, gorgeous, twirly-swirly eyes. "Oh, wow. This is the cutest rat I've ever seen."

"B ..." said Mac, still scared stiff by Slippers.

"If we bulldoze this place it'll mean bulldozing this little guy," said Dave. "And its whole cute rat family. How could we do that? I mean, look at its lovely, big, hypnotic rat eyes. Oh my..."

From behind the trees, Noke gave us a thumbs-up.

Jordan gave a thumbs-up in response. And in this fantastic moment we realised we might have found a way to stop the park getting destroyed. I almost forgot my tummy ache.

Until Coffee Woman returned.

And ruined everything.

C☕FFEE W⚙MAN
STRIKES BACK

Coffee Woman had yet another fresh coffee in her hand.

I'm not sure if she saw us or chose to ignore us as we stayed hidden behind the bench, but she marched around to the far side of the bulldozerbots and stopped to look at the scene.

"Why is this park still here?" she asked.

My face went grey.

So did Melody's.

I clutched her hand tighter.

She gripped tighter still.

"It's OK," Jordan told his sister, but I could tell he wasn't sure of that at all.

Even Poochy, Mr Piggles and Killer seemed

to know this was bad. They had gone quiet
and still.

Coffee Woman approached a bulldozerbot and
ran her finger along the vacuum cleaner tube with
the toilet plunger on it, to where it ended rather
strangely in midair.

She tapped the tube with the bottom of
her coffee cup. Then she tipped the cup over,
emptying coffee all over Sucky's camouflaged
head.

With a crackle of sparks, the robot octopus
flickered into view, then disappeared again,
before, after one last rapid flicker, Sucky lost
all camouflage and was just a broken octobot,
stretched between the diggers.

Sucky was gripping both bulldozerbots with
tentacles stretched to almost breaking point
between them while also holding on to the closest
tree.

Carefully, Coffee Woman prised one tentacle

free. Unable to hold on to the bulldozerbots any longer, Sucky whipped away like a snapped elastic band and flew backwards into the mushy, empty pond.

Next, Coffee Woman walked to Mac, still petrified under Slippers the bear's open jaws.

"B …" he said.

"Bedroom shoes," she said, pointing down.

Mac looked fearfully at Slippers's feet.

"Slippers?" he said.

"I don't think you have much to be scared of. Unless you have a great fear of animals in

comfortable shoes."

"Hee-haw," said Slippers, turning to mosey back along the grass.

Finally, Coffee Woman approached the secret weapon.

She took Herman the hypno-hamster from Dave's hand.

She stared at Herman.

Herman stared back.

"Look at those eyes ..." she said.

Herman's eyes were so big, so shiny, so warm and cute that you couldn't help but love the hamster.

She must have been stunned by Herman's hypnotic cuddliness.

"Such eyes," she said.

She shook Herman.

She shook Herman *very* hard.

Herman's right eye fell out and dangled from a spring.

Dave screamed.

"Shoddy work," she said, and dumped the hamster on the ground. Herman scampered unsteadily towards us. Coffee Woman watched Herman all the way until it found its way back to us.

She didn't wave. Or nod. Or shout. She just smiled a little.

Melody hurriedly pressed Herman's eye back into place.

And that was that. This plan had failed. Just like mine had.

We heard a cracking and rustling in the branches behind us, and the sound of someone arguing with the trees. The complaints sounded very electronic. Very like Noke.

Noke stepped out from the undergrowth, a twig stuck in one ear. "If you have a new skill from your update, now's the time to show us," Noke said to me.

I had no answers.

"Did you learn ninja skills?" asked Noke. "Can you do something explody? You must have *something* you can do now."

I had nothing. No new skills. No old skills. Nothing but a feeling of being broken that went right through me.

We were out of options. There was nothing left to do but watch the park be destroyed.

Except right at that moment, Melody said five words that changed everything.

"I have a tummy ache."

TUMMY TR⚙UBLE

"*I* have a tummy ache," I said.

The men punched commands into the bulldozerbots' keyboards, while Coffee Woman watched, with only occasional glances in our direction. It was as if we didn't matter at all. We were just machines and kids.

"My tummy has felt so broken," I said to Melody. "I've had it since I saw Mr Piggles. And I've felt like there's a fight going on inside me all the time. Sometimes I want to cry, and sometimes I want to laugh, and sometimes it's one after the other."

"Sounds like you, Melody," said Jordan. Annoyed, she slapped her brother weakly on the shoulder.

"I feel very sad even when I should feel happy," I continued. "I feel like shouting and then I feel like not saying anything," I continued.

"I don't want to ruin your big chat about feeling this thing then that thing," said Noke, "but I am *feeling* that those very nasty diggers are destroying everything."

"But it matters," I said to Noke. "Because I had a tummy ache. I thought I was broken. I thought

I was a broken robot. But Melody has the same problem as me. And she's not a robot, And she doesn't look broken to me."

Melody seemed to like that.

"I think I understand," said Jordan. "You've told us about all these things you've been through. Like getting thrown away and escaping the grinder and being lost. That's all going to be hard on anyone's tummy. And head."

I touched my tummy and then my head.

"The feelings keep trying to take over," I said. "There's the bit of my brain that was made to be clever and calm and think things through, but the feelings keep taking over."

"I have that," agreed Melody.

"Oh, I have that too," said Jordan.

"You?" I said.

"Oh yeah. I just hide it better," said Jordan. "You're supposed to feel all that stuff. Just from life. And then all the things you've seen and heard, all those memories, they're part of you now and that can be tough. They'd make anyone ache. Humans have feelings for years and we still find it super hard to control them."

"I'm not broken?" I asked.

"Sounds to me like you're perfectly normal," said Jordan.

The bulldozerbots spluttered and juddered
and then roared as their engines got started again,
ready to wreck the park. It snapped our attention
back on them.

"They're ready to go again, boss," said Mac.
Coffee Woman, without a single glance at us,
stepped back to let it happen.

"You're absolutely, positively, one hundred per
cent sure you have no new skills to help us?" asked
Noke.

My screen began to shine brighter again. A
sunny orange smile rose on my face.

"I have an idea," I shouted as loud as my
childish voice could over the noise of the
bulldozerbots. "My memories. You said it, Jordan.
I have them all in here. All the things I've seen and
heard."

"Not another hologram," said Noke. "A
hologram wouldn't stop a butterfly."

"Not a hologram," I said, looking up at the

giant screen on the building that looked over the park, with its non-stop adverts playing. Right now there was a woman eating cheese. *Mmmm cheese*, said the words across the screen.

"There's one memory I *have* to share with the world. I need to go back on to the internet."

The bulldozerbots had started to churn through soil, munching up roots, causing trees to tip and twist and collapse into each other, exhausted. The

diggers tore a hole in the bushes and revealed the flaky, rusted railings and the city street behind.

Melody stepped in front of the bench and yelled, "Stop it!"

The bulldozer bots did not stop it.

"Noke, I'm going to need your help."

With a crack of chunky fingers, Noke stepped forward. "Do you want to be Monkey Boot or Baby Boot?"

I flashed an exclamation mark where my eyes should be.

"Only joking!" said Noke, and with a tap of my face sent me in to the internet.

THE BIG SCREEN

I was in that strange
tunnel again, a multi-coloured
flow of information and pictures
and words, games and emojis, music
and dancing. A tunnel with countless
tunnels off it, like the branches reaching out
from the trunk of a tree.
This was the internet.
My body was still behind the bench, but my
mind was flying through this incredible
place. It felt so real. So awesome.
So strange.

I *had* to concentrate. I had to focus. I had to ignore all this multi-coloured wonder, no matter how hard it was.

I had to find my way to the huge screen.

I pictured it in my mind, wrapped around the side of the building, and just as I thought about it, the screen flashed by at the end of one of the small tunnels.

"Stop," I said to myself.

Back in the park, where my body was, I could hear the scrunch of soil being dug up by the bulldozerbots. The snap of branches being cut. The creak of a tree falling.

That fear pushed up inside me again, a tight ball sinking like a rock in my tummy. I sensed my emotions trying to take over, trying to get me to drop to the ground and just give up and let them eat me up with the bulldozerbots.

I had to block that out. To concentrate. To keep my mind in the tunnel, in the internet, and steer myself to that screen before it was too late.

I told all those fears and emotions that they could come into my head. That it was OK. That I wasn't going to push them away any more.

I was going to use them. They were part of me. A good part of me.

Emotions are OK.

Being scared was OK.

If I wasn't scared, then I couldn't be brave.

I found the screen again, down that tunnel, like it was a twig on the end of a long branch.

And I went inside it.

"Look at that!" I heard Jordan say.

They all looked up. Noke, Jordan, Melody, Slippers, Poochy ...

Coffee Woman.

They watched the giant screen blink and the ad for the coffee shops burst on to it. Coffee Woman appeared in it, just as always. She held up her coffee and winked.

The screen blinked again.

Coffee Woman reappeared.

She wasn't smiling this time.

She was scowling.

She was in the coat, in the park. Just as I had seen her. Just as the whole city was about to see her.

I replayed the memory of her from earlier on.

"Stop!" I heard her shout.

The bulldozerbots stopped.

The digging stopped.

But I didn't.

AD BREAK

Coffee Woman was on the screen, her snarl taking up three storeys of the building.

"*People only care about their morning coffee. People only care about stuffing their faces with cakes. They only care about eating and drinking and spending money.*"

People stopped on the street below. They looked away from the smaller screens on their robots and up to the giant one on the building above.

"*Why should they care about this park?*" Coffee Woman was shouting at them.

"*If they want animals they can see them on the internet or in the zoo or they can buy pretend ones and throw them out when they're bored.*"

From the park, Coffee Woman tried to scramble over the railings.

"Don't look at the woman on the screen!" she
screamed.

Her coat caught on a spike and after trying to
free it a couple of times she just tore it loose.

"*People. Are. Idiots,*" she boomed from the huge
screen.

"I didn't say that," she insisted, going from

person to person on the street.

"*Idiots,*" she said again.

The relentless bustle of this part of the city had calmed completely while people stopped and stared up, heads back, hands shading eyes, mouths open.

"*They don't care about anything but looking at screens and spending money ...*"

People started pointing at the torn bushes, through which she'd scrambled. On the other side of the gap they could see the yellow of the bulldozerbots, their blades dirty with the soil they'd been digging up.

"*People won't even notice your precious park is gone unless someone puts it on a screen for them.*"

"Unplug that screen!" she demanded.

I played the memory again, feeling myself tiring.

I heard a loud, deep hum rising across the streets. Was it another bulldozerbot? Something worse?

No, I realised. It was the people of the city. They had spotted the park and the hole torn through its trees. They had spotted Coffee Woman.

"That's ... that's *her*!" yelled someone.

"Is she tearing up that park?" someone else asked.

"Did she call us idiots?" asked another. "*I'm* not an idiot."

I couldn't stay online much longer. I played the message for as long as I could, but started to lose control. The screen flickered. The memory glitched.

I stopped playing it.

Frozen on the screen was a picture of her face, reddened with anger, her coffee spilling from the cup, her knuckles white with fury, as it glitched "*idiots ... idiots ... idiots ...* " over and over and over before finally fading away.

I left the internet.

I was thrown back down the tunnel, whooshing

through the churning information, until I landed
back in my own head with such force that my
body fell over.

I lay on the ground in the park, looking up at
faces.

Jordan, Melody, Noke. Mr Piggles, Poochy.
Killer. Sucky. Slippers, with Herman peeking out
from one of the bear's slippers.

And all around them, so many more faces of all
the people flooding in from the street, intrigued
and amazed and saying:

"I didn't know this park was here."

and

"This is beautiful. Was someone really trying to tear it up?"

and

"Why would anyone do that? We can't let that happen."

And one very alarmed voice in particular asking:

"Is that a *bear*?"

Dave and Mac from the wrecking crew sat on the bench, helmets tipped back as they scratched their heads.

"What do we do now?" asked Dave.

"Dunno," said Mac.

"I really fancy a cream bun," said Dave.

"Me too," said Mac.

They stood and with a press of buttons turned the bulldozerbots around and sent them rumbling harmlessly across the park towards the exit.

TW✸ DAYS LATER

PARK LIFE

The sun shone.

It shone through the gap in the buildings so I felt its energy reach every corner of every wire and pixel in my body.

It shone on the signs people had made and hung up all over the park.

SAVE IVY PARK.

LEAVE THE TREES ALONE.

STOP SQUASHING SQUIRRELS!

It shone on the people wandering through and

enjoying this oasis of green in the city. Many had children with them and were tying ribbons around tree trunks, ribbons of all colours.

It shone on Beth and me, sitting on the bench watching life filling the park.

Jordan and Melody waved at us from where they had stretched some ribbons around an area of grass. Melody had written a sign that said: PET CORNER, and was encouraging people to put their pets – real and robot – in there while their owners enjoyed the park.

People didn't pay much attention to Mr Piggles, Killer and the rest of the pets. They were just a few robot pets among many brought to the park.

There was a tiny giraffe. A cat in pyjamas. A lizard with a big frilly neck that flashed amazing patterns of colours.

"RUFF," barked Poochy, jumping up and down in response to the lizard's light show. "RUFFZZZPPPTTT."

A man sat on the grass by the edge of the pond, now refilled with water. He put a green lolly in his mouth. When a pair of octopus eyes peered out of the water, the man's mouth dropped open and he just held the lolly on his tongue, which got greener and greener as his mouth got wider and wider.

Sucky popped out of the water and disappeared in the time it took for the man's lolly to slip off his tongue and on to the grass.

Beth laughed. My face was a sunny orange of happiness too.

"I didn't even know this place was here," I heard one person say to a friend as she walked by. "But I'm so glad it is."

"Me too," said her friend. "I wonder if there's anywhere we can get a coffee here."

My smile sank a bit.

"Don't worry about it," said Beth. "Everything is going to be OK. They're not knocking down this park, thanks to you and your new friends. But after all the excitement, how are you feeling?"

How was I feeling?

I checked, concentrated on my mind, my tummy, looked for all the clues to see how I was feeling right now.

I was feeling happy that the sun was out and we were here in a beautiful park that had been saved.

I was feeling relieved that I wasn't broken.

I was feeling a bit sad about the damage done by the bulldozerbots and that Grandma couldn't be here.

I was feeling hopeful that the amazing, fantastic, incredible life I saw in this park could be saved and stay in this place for ever.

I was feeling a little scared about what might happen next.

I was feeling worried for the pets that they would be OK hiding here.

I was feeling pleased that they had kind and selfless humans looking after them.

I was feeling excited for whatever adventures we had ahead of us.

I was feeling grateful to have the best friends I could ever ask for, whether they were robots or humans, and that I had a home. No, *two* homes now.

I was feeling surprise no. 300 at how, so soon

after all seemed broken, the world felt green and marvellous and hopeful again.

I was feeling …

… everything. All the feelings. All in there, sometimes working well together, sometimes one fighting to take over.

But they were part of who I was. Part of being *me*.

ACKN●WLEDGMENTS

Thanks to Ben Mantle for bringing Boot and pals to life with his awesome illustrations.

Thanks to Rachel Wade for being a fantastic editor.

Thank you to everyone at Hachette for bringing Boot to the readers, including Hilary Murray Hill, Ruth Alltimes, Kate Agar, Samuel Perrett, Lucy Clayton, Emily Finn, Nicola Goode, Anne McNeil, Valentina Fazio, Siobhán Tierney and Elaine Egan.

Thanks to my agent, the endlessly amazing Marianne Gunn O'Connor, and to Michelle Kroes in CAA, Los Angeles.

Special thanks to Maeve, Oisín, Caoimhe, Aisling and Laoise, who are always the first to go on Boot's adventures. Thanks to my mum and dad Tim and Marie and my sisters Niamh and Anne.

Thank you to all the booksellers, librarians and teachers bringing great books to young people everywhere. And thanks to all of you brilliant readers who have made sharing Boot's stories so much fun.

Join BOOT on a dangerous adventure to find where home is, what friends look like, and why humans are so leaky and weird.

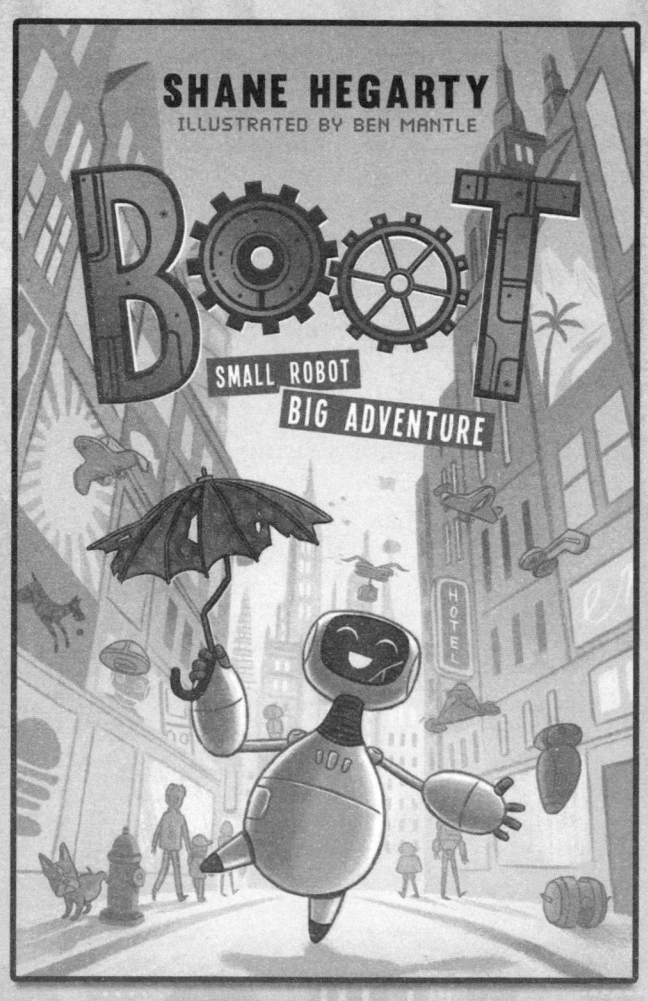